LOVING THE

Biker

CASSIE ALEXANDRA

MORE BOOKS

by CASSIE ALEXANDRA

Resisting the Biker
Surviving the Biker
Fearing the Biker
Breaking the Biker
Taming the Biker
Loving the Biker

by K.L. MIDDLETON

Tangled Beauty
Tangled Mess
Tangled Fury
Sharp Edges

bestselling romance author

bad • boy • romances

One

TERIN

"**Y**OU ARE GOING to be there, right?"

"Of course," I said, setting my keys and gun down onto the kitchen counter. "I'd never miss my own sister's bachelorette party."

"Not deliberately, but I know how involved you are with work, and lately things seem to be slipping your mind."

"I told you before, I didn't forget about the fitting appointment," I replied, walking over to the refrigerator. I opened it and grabbed a container of leftover pepperoni and mushroom pizza. "I was held up in court."

"You could have at least sent me a text," scolded my younger sister, Torie. "We waited around for you for over an hour."

I snorted.

Yeah, that would have gone over well.

"I was on the witness stand. I couldn't ask the judge for a 'texting break'," I replied, picturing Judge Cornweather's reaction to a request like that. He was a cynical, ornery, old goat who had little patience for any kind of courtroom interruptions. Pausing in the middle of my questioning to send a message would have given him an aneurism.

"I know." She sighed. "At least we're the same size and was able to stand in for you at the fitting. Have you tried the dress on yet?"

"Yes," I answered.

"So, what do you think?"

"Not bad."

She gasped. "What do you mean, not bad?"

"It's nice," I replied, putting the pizza in the microwave.

"But not beautiful or gorgeous. You hate it."

"For God's sake, I don't hate it." I should have known she'd overreact. Torie had always been sensitive, and this wedding was giving her so much anxiety that even she couldn't wait for it to be over.

"Is it the color?"

The dresses were dark red and made of satin. Honestly, I didn't mind the color. What I minded was the plunging neckline, which showed more cleavage than I was comfortable with. I wasn't going to tell her that, however. It was her wedding and I wanted my younger sister to be happy. She'd fallen in love with the dresses and I wasn't going to make a fuss. "Torie, you know how I feel about wearing dresses in general. They're just not my thing."

"What if I told you that I was getting married just to see you get into one?" she said, a smile in her voice.

"I'd say that was a costly decision and you could have just paid me the money directly," I replied, grinning.

She laughed. "Damn, *now* you tell me?"

Torie adored her fiancé, Tom, and had always dreamed of getting married ever since she was old enough to play with Barbie dolls. They were both realtors and full of energy. They'd also just started their own business of buying shitty homes to renovate and resell. They seemed to have the ideal relationship, which worried me. In my line of work, their life seemed too good to be true and Tom, a little too 'perfect'.

"I think you can still get your deposit back on the banquet hall if you want to cancel," I teased.

"You wish," she replied, taking a drink from her cup. "You'd love to see me leave Tom hanging at the altar."

"Now *why* would you say that?" I asked innocently.

"You think he has skeletons in his closet."

Yes, my sister knows me well.

"He sends you flowers every Friday, draws your baths, reads you books, and cooks these amazing gourmet meals. Are you sure he isn't gay?"

"Why would you say that?"

"Because gay men are so thoughtful and know how to pamper their partners."

"How would you know?" she asked.

"Ricky." My old roommate had been gay. He'd moved to Florida a couple of years ago, and I missed him dearly. We still talked on the phone, but only a couple times a year. He'd been one of my best friends and had given me a lot of advice about men.

"Oh yeah. How is he these days?"

"Good. The last I heard he was opening up his own fitness club."

"Tell him 'hi' the next time you talk to him."

"I will. Anyway, back to Tom. You know I love you and only want what's best. He just seems so... I don't know... flawless."

"You're just cynical about men. I don't blame you, since you obviously deal with sociopaths all day long. Seriously though, Tom is by no means perfect."

"Right. He gives your cat 'massages'."

"Tom says that it releases cytokines, which in turn releases natural painkilling chemicals and is good for the digestion, too."

"Of course he would know that," I mused.

"Being a cop, I'd think you'd be happy that I found a good guy," she said sternly.

"I am happy. If he is a good guy. I mean, I certainly want him to be." I sighed. "I guess you're right. I'm cynical and paranoid. I don't want anyone hurting my little sister."

"I love you, too."

"Thank you."

"You know what you need?" she asked. "You need some cytokines released. When was the last time you slept with anyone or had your kitty massaged?"

Removing the pizza from the microwave, I thought about Jason, the last guy I'd had sex with. I'd met him at the gym. He was a lawyer and seemed to have had all of his shit together. After going out with him a couple of times, we ended up in his bed, and although it hadn't been mind-blowing, I'd enjoyed it. What I hadn't enjoyed was finding out that he was married and the way it happened. His wife, who was apparently concerned about the amount of time he'd been spending at the gym, hired a private investigator. After finding out he'd been cheating, she shot him in the thigh. He'd survived, but it had been such a harrowing experience that I wasn't in a hurry to jump into bed with anyone else.

"How do you know I haven't been getting laid?" I asked, shoving a piece of pepperoni into my mouth.

"Please. You're not the only one who studies people, you know. There's a reason why I sold seven expensive homes last month," she replied. "Anyway, there's going to be a lot of hot guys at the wedding. Some are wealthy realtors who make more in a month than you probably make all year. Just think, you can marry one of them, quit your job, and not have to worry about catching bad guys anymore."

"I like catching the bad guys," I replied, offended. "And... I'm making decent money now. In fact, I was just transferred to the Street Gang Unit in Jensen." There were actually three teams. The Suppression Teams, Graffiti Strike Force, and Gang Investigations. I was part of Investigations.

"That's what mom told me," she said. "Does that mean you're going to be butting heads with the Gold Vipers?"

"You could say that," I replied, having already gone through some of the club's records. Their president, Slammer Fleming, had recently been murdered, which was one of the reasons why I'd been transferred to the unit. Between the Gold Vipers and their rivals, the Devil's Rangers, bodies were piling up and the task force needed more manpower.

"They're not all bad guys," said Torie, as if reading my mind. "In fact, I know Tank. I think he's the V.P now."

"He's been recently promoted to President," I said, frowning. "And what do you mean, you know him?"

"We graduated high school together," she said. "And, I went out with him once."

My eye twitched.

Our father, a man who'd spent thirty years of his life as a cop, had to be rolling over in his grave right about now.

"Hello? Terin?"

11

"I wasn't aware of that. Did mom know?" I replied, no longer hungry. I shoved the food away, went to the refrigerator and took out a beer.

"No. She wouldn't have understood."

"That's an understatement. I can't believe you dated a thug."

"He's not a thug. At least, he wasn't back then. Honestly," she chuckled. "It wasn't the worst date I've ever had, either. The guy was hot – and talk about funny. I remember laughing so hard that I almost peed my pants at the restaurant."

"Good thing there was only one date with Mr. Comedian."

I'd learned that one of Tank's girlfriends had been murdered three years ago. A girl by the name of Krystal Blake. We suspected that it was her death that actually triggered an all-out war between the Gold Vipers and the Devil's Rangers. Now there were four dead men linked to both clubs, including Jon Hughes, the last Devil's Ranger's Mother charter president. Slammer was the most recent death, however, and we knew that there'd be more retaliation.

"He isn't a bad guy. I'm telling you."

I rolled my eyes. Torie was so naïve. "Maybe not back then, but his club is definitely involved in some major criminal activity."

"Like what?"

I took a sip of my beer and licked my lips. "You know that I can't get into it with you. But... let's just say if you're on the Gold Vipers' bad side, moving to another country would be a wise choice," I said, saying more than I was supposed to. But, she was my sister and I needed her to know the truth. "Or buying life insurance."

"Really? They do so much for the community. They even donated a large chunk of money to this Cancer Awareness Benefit that I helped host last summer. Slammer, Justin's father, donated over ten grand. He's a generous man."

"He is also deceased."

She sucked in her breath. "Really? That's horrible. When did it happen?"

"About four weeks ago. I take it you didn't see it on the news?"

"I haven't had a lot of time to *watch* the news." She sighed. "That's too bad. He was so funny. I met him and his wife Frannie, during the benefit. They seemed like such a nice couple."

"You do realize that the money he donated to your benefit was dirty."

"You don't know that for sure. He had a legitimate business," said Torie.

"Oh, you mean that strip joint?" I snickered. "What's the name? Oh yeah, Griffin's. That place is a cesspool of drug dealers, junkies, and hookers. They've

13

busted some of the girls who work there for prostitution and drug possession."

"It's a strip joint. I guess that I'm not surprised. Look, I'm just saying that the Justin I knew, back in school, was sweet and I can't imagine him being a murderer."

"I'm not saying that he is either. But, the Gold Vipers, in general, are bad news."

"I hear you. Anyway, enough about them. I just wanted to make sure you're going to be at my bachelorette party."

"When is it again? Friday?"

"No, Saturday," she replied. "I've told you several times. Please, don't tell me you have to work."

"I have it off and don't worry, I'll be there."

"Good. A party bus is going to be picking us up at eight. My place. Don't be late."

A party bus sounded too confining and the thought of being shut in with a bunch of drunk, hell-raising women was already giving me a headache. "Why don't I just meet you at one of the bars? I'm not going to drink anyway."

"Bullshit. You're drinking and you're going to let loose and have a good time, even if it kills you."

I took another swig of beer. "This is your party. I don't need to let loose."

"You're right. It is my party, and if you don't arrive at my place, before eight, dressed to kill and ready to get your freak on, I swear to God... I'm going to make the holidays hell for you. I'll even make you pick up Aunt Dottie from the airport this year."

Our great aunt was annoying, rude, and bossy. Not only did she complain about everything and everybody, but she had the mouth of a sailor. I could only stand so much of her rantings, and the thought of spending time alone with her was enough to make my eye twitch.

"Fine. I'll be there," I mumbled.

"I knew you would," she replied, a smile in her voice.

"You're such a bitch."

"Thank you. Everything I learned was from my big sister," she said. "But, we both know I have nothing on her."

I grinned. She was probably right.

Two

COLE

I PULLED INTO the gates of the clubhouse and parked my Hog next to Tank's. He was standing beside it and talking to my sister, Raina, who was now his Old Lady. She smiled at me and I winked back.

"Hey, Prez," I said, taking off my brain bucket.

"Where've you been, Ice?" he asked me, his face stony. He'd given me the road name the week before, saying that I had an ice-cold stare, almost as bad as my sister's. Of course, Tank could make a grizzly bear shit himself with a single look. He and Raina were definitely made for each other. As petite and vulnerable as she looked, Raina took no B.S. from anyone, including her fiancé.

"I was at the hardware store, picking up a new motor for the garbage disposal," I said, opening up one of the saddlebags on my bike. I pulled the part out and held it up. "Hopefully this will work."

Tank frowned. "It took two hours?"

I wanted to tell him that he sounded like my fucking ex, Patty. Always questioning and nagging me. But I held my tongue. I was just a prospect and it went with the territory.

"No. Hoss sent me over to his place to pick up his cell phone," I said, reaching into my jeans pocket. I

17

pulled it out and showed him. "He also wanted me to feed his fish and that crazy fucking dog of his."

Hoss, the club's Sergeant-At-Arms, owned a Pitbull and the dog almost ripped off my nuts the moment I'd walked through the front door. When I'd agreed to feed the damn thing, I had no idea he owned a Pit, which I knew were very territorial. Needless to say, the dog made it abundantly clear that I wasn't wanted, even after I filled his bowl with food and gave him fresh water. I was still a stranger invading his property and he wasn't one to take a bribe.

"Homer?" asked Tank, breaking into a smile. "And you made it out of there alive?"

I wasn't about to tell him that I'd kept a bat between me and the dog, so I played it cool. "Yeah. I just had to show him who's boss."

Chuckling, Tank glanced at Raina. "I'm impressed. Your brother has some massive balls, darlin', and Homer usually eats those for breakfast."

"Why does Hoss own such a mean dog?" she asked. Raina didn't know much about dogs in general, although my nephew, Billy, had been begging her for a puppy.

"He's only mean to strangers. Homer was beaten as a puppy and Hoss rescued him. The dog is still pretty skittish around people he doesn't see very often, even when Hoss is home. But he loves that old man and would die for him."

Raina looked horrified. "How can anyone beat a puppy? There are a lot of sick assholes in this world."

"Damn right there is. Especially in this town, which is another reason why I think you should join Jessica's Tae Kwon Do class. You two can learn how to defend yourselves and get to know each other more in the process."

"Isn't she in Vegas, still?" asked Raina, running a hand through her dark hair. "With Jordan?"

"Yeah. I spoke to her last night though. It sounds as if they'll be returning Sunday," said Tank.

"Those two get hitched out there?" I asked him. They'd been gone for three weeks, which was a little surprising, considering it was Vegas. As far as I was concerned, there wasn't much to do in Sin City but gamble, go to strip clubs, and party. Something for a weekend, not twenty-one days, and definitely not with a chick.

"I asked her and she said that they didn't," said Tank. "Which is good because I'm pretty sure Frannie would flip her lid. She wants Jessica to have a big wedding with the family."

"Three weeks now. Wow," said Raina. "That can't be cheap."

"Hell, he's got money stashed somewhere," said Tank. "Anyway, they originally went out there for business and decided to stay longer. I think she said that they rented a house."

"You sure they didn't get married?" asked Raina, smiling. "And are just saving the news for when they get back?"

"It's possible, but knowing Jessica, she'd also want a big wedding. On the other hand," he scratched his chin, "I doubt that Jordan would agree to that."

I'd heard rumors that Jordan Steele, Raptor's brother, was the infamous "Judge." When I'd asked Tank about it, however, he'd only laughed and brushed it off.

"Why is that?" I asked, curious. I, myself, never planned on getting married, but if I had to, I'd opt for a small church wedding in town and a big party afterward at Sal's, my uncle's bar.

"He's a quiet guy. Isn't very sociable either," said Tank. He looked at Raina. "Hell, I was surprised he even showed up for dinner that night, before they went on their trip."

"He did look a little uncomfortable," mused Raina.

"What about you two?" I asked. "You set a date yet?"

"Not yet," said Raina, giving me the look. The one that said to drop the subject. I knew Tank was pushing for a wedding harder than she was. But, she'd been married before and wasn't in any kind of rush to walk down the aisle again.

I shoved Hoss's small phone back into the front of my jeans. "You having a big church wedding?"

"Yes," said Tank.

"No," said Raina, at the same time.

They looked at each other.

He put his arm over her shoulders. "Baby, you know that I'll do whatever you want, but... I gotta tell you... the guys expect a big hoopla of a wedding. So does Frannie."

Raina's first wedding had turned out to be much more expensive than originally planned. She always said that if she had to do it over again, she'd elope.

"We'll talk about it later," said Raina.

"Sure." Tank looked back at me. "By the way, Ice, we have church at two. I want you there today."

In the past, I hadn't been invited to many of the weekly meetings, so this was surprising. In general, Prospects were not privy to a lot of the private matters. I had a feeling that me being a former Devil's Ranger made them even more tight-lipped. I understood why, but it was a little disconcerting.

"Sounds good. I'll be there," I said, curious as to why I'd been invited.

With his arm still around Raina, he pulled her away from the bike and the couple headed toward the clubhouse. "Hoss's inside... probably on Facebook," he said, over his shoulder.

I snorted.

Hoss had recently set up an account and was already addicted. He was "friending" everyone and getting messages from women in all parts of the world, some of them "enthralled with his handsome photo." Hoss wasn't a bad looking guy, and I imagined that if he bathed more and lost a few inches around his beer gut, in turn... he might attract women here in town. But, he seemed to be intrigued with the ones online.

We'd all tried to warn him about scam artists, but Hoss insisted that the women messaging him were the real deal. That they liked bikers, even ones old enough to be their grandfather.

I followed Tank and Raina into the clubhouse and sought out Hoss. He was sitting at the bar alone and on his laptop.

"Here's your cell phone," I said, noticing that he was on Facebook again.

"Thanks. How's Homer?" He held out his hand and I gave it to him.

"Fine. Thanks for the warning," I said dryly.

He laughed hoarsely. "You wouldn't have gone over there if I'd have told you the truth."

"Sure I would have. But I'd have been more prepared to face 'Cerberus',"' I said, staring at his screen.

He gave me a confused look. "Cerberus?"

"It's from Greek mythology. Cerberus was the hound of Hades. Who the fuck is Lana?"

"This chick from Florida. She has the hots for me," he said, smiling proudly. "Hell, she thinks she loves me. Can't say I blame her."

I sighed. "Love? Really? You've gotta be shitting me...."

His face darkened. "What?"

"Think about it. Lana claims to be in love with you. Already. You don't find that fishy?" I replied, watching as he began typing a message to a blond, twenty-something hottie who had sent him a picture of herself in black lingerie. Her looks alone told me that she was up to something.

"We've been messaging each other now for the last three days," he explained. "She claims that she has feelings for me. I've seen guys around here fall for a chick in less time than that."

Still frowning, I shook my head. "Jesus, you know, 'she' is probably really a 'he'... and one of those romance scammers."

"A what?"

"It was on the news a while back. Basically, it's the same-old shit. People getting swindled out of money by assholes who pretend to be someone they're not. They prey mostly on lonely people."

"I'm not lonely, although most of my best friends *are* six feet under now," he said, looking me out of the corner of his eye.

Ouch. Talk about cutting in deep.

"I'm sorry," I said softly, feeling like shit. The shame of knowing I'd been a part of that was sometimes enough to make me want to walk out of the clubhouse and never return. I'm not sure what held me back from doing just that, though. Maybe I was looking for a way to redeem myself. Or, maybe I was doing it for Raina. All I knew for sure was that we both had our own demons to conquer when it came to Slammer.

Hoss didn't respond right away. He pulled out a cigarette and stuck it into his mouth. "Whether you're sorry or not, isn't going to change anything. Isn't going to bring him back."

"Hoss–"

Hoss held up his hand. "Hey, I can't have this conversation with you," he said, his voice hard. "I want you to know, however, that I don't hold you personally responsible. You feel me?"

All I could do was nod.

"Shit happened and it's over," he continued, as if trying to convince himself of it more than me. "We can move beyond it or hold grudges."

I could tell that he wasn't finished, so I remained quiet.

"I guess that if Tank can find it in his heart to forgive you, then I'm willing to do the same. I just… don't want to talk about it. Wounds are still too fresh."

"I understand," I replied.

He removed the unlit cigarette from his mouth and sniffed along the edge. "Damn, I miss these things. Almost as much as beaver."

"You quit?"

He gave me a shit-eating grin. "One I did. The other I'm hoping to get from blondie, here. Haven't had me a fine piece of ass like that in a long time."

"I'm telling you, watch out for that chick."

"I am watching," he said, clicking through the sexy pictures on her page. "And I like what I see."

I noticed Raptor walk into the room with Chopper, the Intelligence Officer.

"Hey. What's up?" asked Raptor, stepping over to us.

"Hoss thinks he's met the girl of his dreams," I said, smirking.

"I don't know about the girl of my dreams, but I'd love to make hers come true by slipping her the old Hoss Special," joked Hoss.

Chopper and I laughed.

"Old man, you'd better calm yourself before you go popping more blood vessels in your eyes," said Raptor, patting him on the shoulder.

"That happened because of my contacts," said Hoss, giving him a dirty look. "Not from jacking off. I told you that, fucker."

Raptor laughed. "So touchy. You quit smoking again?"

"Yeah. As a matter of fact I did," said Hoss.

"How's that going?" asked Raptor.

"Not so good, especially when I'm reminded of it," said Hoss.

"Candy helps," I said, itching to have a cigarette myself. I'd been trying to cut back because I was broke, and even that was hell.

"I heard that, too. Should have had you pick me up some," said Hoss. "Or gum. You try that nicotine gum?"

"No," I said.

He pulled out a piece and unwrapped it. "I've been chewing on them for the last couple of days. Seems to take the edge off, I guess."

"So, who are we looking at?" asked Chopper, leaning over Hoss's shoulder.

"Lana. She wants to hook up," said Hoss.

"With *you*?" asked Raptor in disbelief.

"Yeah, with me, dickhead."

"Isn't she kind of young for you?" asked Chopper.

"No. She's old enough. In fact, Lana is a college student, living in Florida. She's been living off of soup and macaroni-and-cheese for the last year. Ice thinks she's lying but I don't know. I mean, it sounds legitimate," he said, waving his hand at the screen.

"Are you fucking kidding me?" said Chopper as he read the last message she sent to him, a dark expression on his face. "That chick says she loves you and is willing to fly over... *if* she had the money. Emphasis on 'if'. You don't see anything wrong with that?"

"Not really. College students are always broke. Nothing unusual about that," he said matter-of-factly.

"What's unusual is she wants to hook up with you," joked Chopper.

Hoss flipped him off.

"She wants to hook him, not hook up," said Raptor. "You'd better be careful, Hoss. I'm serious."

"Eh. I haven't given her my credit card number or anything like that. It's been innocent flirting. Like I told Ice, we've been chatting for the last few days."

Raptor stared at him in disbelief. "Chatting? Come on, Hoss. You know better, brother. That's a fucking set-up if I've ever seen one. She's waiting for you to tell her that you'll pay for her flight and maybe more. Then you'll wire her money and never hear from her again."

Hoss began to look a little uncertain. "I think you're wrong. She says she loves bikers."

"Right," said Raptor dryly "Tell me this, if she looks like that, why would she need to date strangers on the internet?"

"She's tired of the guys in her town? I don't know. She hasn't asked me for money. Here, watch this." He began typing her a message that said he'd drive down to Florida on his Hog and they could have dinner together, if she really wanted to see him.

Raptor and I both looked at each other, matching expressions on our faces.

"You're wrong about Lana. Just wait and see," said Hoss, grinning as he added a heart to the message. "She's going to be fucking thrilled when she reads this." He hit *SEND* and sent the message.

"This should be interesting," said Raptor with a wry smile. He pointed to the screen. "Oh, look. It shows that she's read your message already."

Less than twenty seconds later, Lana responded and stated that she was thinking about moving to Iowa and would rather come out to see him.

"Well that's even better," said Hoss. His smile fell when he read the next line.

"I hate to say 'I told you so'," said Raptor. "But, she's asking you to loan her the money. And, well, would you look at that? She'll even pay you back when she gets here."

"Why can't she just pay for the ticket herself then?" wondered Hoss out loud.

"Because it's a scam," said Raptor. "That's how these fuckers steal your money."

Hoss's face turned red. "That bitch. I should drive down to Florida and really give her a piece of my fucking mind. I guess *her* beauty isn't skin deep."

Raptor and I looked at each other again.

He just didn't get it.

Hoss still thought the sexy girl on the photo was still the scammer.

"This is why I stay off of social media," said Chopper. "Everyone is after something. It's unsafe." He looked at Raptor. "Speaking of which, you want me to check our computer? Find out why it's running so slowly?"

"That would be great. It's actually Adriana's. She's been having some problems."

"I've got time right now. Should we head over to your place?" he asked.

"Sounds good," he replied.

"See you later," muttered Hoss, still staring at his computer screen.

"Why don't you get off the computer and go take a walk? It's a beautiful day," said Chopper. "Get some fresh air into your lungs."

"Who are you now? Dr. Oz?" asked Hoss.

"Very funny. You won't be laughing when your accounts get hacked because you're not playing it safe on the internet."

Hoss ignored him.

"Your stubbornness is your worst enemy," said Chopper.

"No, his dick is," said Raptor. "And he's thinking with it."

"I'm not going to let her swindle me," said Hoss, looking up. "So just chill out."

"Whatever you do, *don't* send her any money," warned Raptor, walking away with Chopper. "You'll never see it again."

"Don't worry. I won't," said Hoss, pulling the cigarette out of his pocket again. This time, he took out his lighter too.

"Don't do it," I said, nodding toward the cigarette.

"Fuck," he growled, shoving them back into his pockets.

"I'd better go and fix the disposal. Don't forget, the meeting is at two," I told him.

"I know. How did you hear about it?" he asked, typing again.

"Tank asked me to be there."

Hoss looked up. "*You*? Why?"

I shrugged. "I don't know."

He looked perplexed. "You're just a Prospect."

"I know."

He sat back in his chair. "You've only been here two months."

"Yeah. Maybe he's allowing Prospects into the meetings now."

As if on cue, one of the other Prospects, Dover, walked into the clubhouse carrying two buckets of paint.

"Tank invite you to the meeting, Dover?" Hoss asked him.

"What meeting?" replied Dover.

"Forget about it," mumbled Hoss. He didn't say another word and went back to his typing.

"What meeting?" repeated Dover, this time looking at me.

"Don't worry about it," I said, leaving the room. I went into the small kitchen in the clubhouse and began to fix the garbage disposal.

You're just a Prospect...

Obviously, Hoss had forgotten that they'd all been one of those at one time or another. Yeah, I was a Prospect and damn good at it, too. Hell, I'd pretty much hit the ground running when Tank announced he was sponsoring me, wanting to not only make up for the shit that had happened, but also prove how committed I was to club. The grunt work, midnight errands, and wild goose chases were bad enough, but now they had me scrubbing toilets, mowing lawns, and feeding killer dogs. And hell, I did everything without batting an eye, but there were times that I wondered if they'd ever patch me.

Hoss.

I respected the guy but it was obvious that he was having a hard time accepting the turn of events. Sometimes I'd see him watching me silently, his eyes stormy and his jaw tight. He and Slammer had been best friends, from what I'd learned. Closer than any other brothers in the club. A loss like that would be felt for the rest of your days. And then there was Tank.

Although he was sponsoring me as a new Prospect for the Gold Vipers, and was about to marry my sister, there was still an awkward tension between us. The reason was obvious... I'd driven his father's killer, my sister, Raina, to-and-from the crime scene. He'd found it in his heart to forgive her for killing his old man, because she'd believed he'd been the one responsible for ordering the drive-by that had almost killed her two-year-old son. Pulling the trigger on Slammer had been a crime of passion. She'd been a grieving mother, her heart and spirit broken. A woman completely undone. Although his pain had been deep, Tank had found a way to forgive her. Me, on the other hand, he owed me nothing. I'd had every chance to turn the van around and stop Slammer's death. The truth was, deep down I didn't think she was going to do it, but she'd surprised the hell out of me. Thinking back now, it almost made me a bigger asshole. Slammer could have wrestled the gun away from Raina, leaving Billy motherless. She was my sister. I should have *never* let her face him alone.

Shouldn't have.

Could have.

Didn't.

I'd heard the words plenty of times out of Uncle Sal's lips, back when I was a young punk. Apparently, I still need a kick in the ass when it came to getting my shit together.

Sighing, I grabbed a wrench.

There was no use dwelling on the past. All I could do was try and make up for it. I only hoped that club would someday forgive and accept me like they would anyone else.

Three

TERIN

"IT'S BEEN FIVE** weeks now since Slammer's homicide," said Daniel Walters, the head of our unit. It was early Monday morning and he looked like he'd been up for two days. The lines on his face were deep and made him look much older than forty. "And we still don't have a damn shooter. We need to start pressing the Gold Vipers for more information."

"You think they really know who killed him?" I asked, but then immediately felt like an idiot when all eight eyes turned toward me.

Walters grunted. "Of course they know. Hell, even *we* know it was the Devil's Rangers."

"Has there been any recent retaliation at all?" I asked. "By the Gold Vipers?"

"Not yet, but there will be," said Jeffrey Bronson, another investigator on the task force. He was stuffing his bloated, puffy face with powdered donuts. Normally, I had no problem with obese men, but this one had 'accidently' groped me in the copy-room the other day. Jeffrey licked the powder from his fingers and grabbed another. "That's what my sources are saying. The Gold Vipers are playing this cool right now. They obviously know we're watching them. But make no mistake, someone is going to pay for murdering Slammer. I'm sure they'll probably even use the Judge again."

"Won't Tank want to do it himself?" I asked, tapping my pen against the notepad in front of me. "Murder the guy who killed his father?"

"He'll want to and maybe he even will, but my informants claim that Slammer always insisted that the club pay someone else to do their dirty work. They keep their noses clean and by using a hit-man like the Judge, they'll stay out of prison," said Bronson, talking with his mouth full.

From what I'd learned, the Judge was a hired hit-man and was pretty much untraceable. Rumor had it that he was used to kill Breaker and also blew up the Devil's Rangers' club in Hayward, Minnesota. Not only did he apparently know what he was doing, but he was a master of disguise. We didn't even have a real description of him. For all we knew, the Judge could be a young woman.

"I have people breathing down my back about this fucking case and they want answers, just as much as I do. So, we need to dig deeper. Even if it means that we grill the Gold Vipers until one of them breaks," said Walters, running a hand over his face.

"We've tried," said Bronson. "In fact, last time we were interrogating one of them, they requested a lawyer and now they're all throwing that in our faces. 'Talk to my fucking lawyer'. That's all I hear now."

"You interrogated one of them just recently?" I asked. "When was that?"

"Just a few days ago. A Prospect named Dover," said Bronson. "Brought him in after his sister's scumbag boyfriend was found beaten to a pulp in the back alley of Sal's. She had bruises on her, too. Nobody is confessing to anything, but it looks like the boyfriend might have knocked her around, and when big brother found out about it, he took matters into his own hands."

"Were there any charges pressed?" asked Walters.

"Of course not. The boyfriend is scared shitless of Dover and his club. Hell, the asshole is lucky that he just got off with a broken nose and a few bruises," replied Bronson.

Walters looked at me. "You haven't met any of them face-to-face yet?"

"No," I replied.

"Maybe we're going about this wrong," said Walters, tapping his thumb against the desk.

"What are you thinking?" asked Bronson, a funny smile on his face. "Send O'Brien over to the clubhouse or maybe Griffins? Have her do some undercover work?"

"Actually, that might not be a bad idea," he replied, scratching his chin.

Fred Gervais, the fifth person in our unit, cleared his throat. "It might not be a good idea, either."

"You have a better one, Fred?" asked Walters, looking irritated.

Fred, who was only a couple years away from retiring, shrugged. "Not really. But, she isn't going to find anything. You know that."

I pictured myself alone and in a biker bar. I'd probably get hit on, but I doubted that any of them would share club information, even *if* they thought they'd get lucky. "Fred is probably right. Even if I came on to one of them, which believe me, isn't going to happen, I doubt they'd share anything. In fact, I'm pretty sure that even the Old Ladies aren't privy to club business."

"Relax. We're not asking you to sleep with any of them. Just start frequenting the places they hang out," he said. "Obviously, you'd be on the clock and getting paid for it."

"What if one of them tries having sex with her?" asked Pen, another detective.

"Oh, I'm sure they will. All she has to do is decline the invitation. This particular club isn't known for violence against women," said Walters. "Anyway, I'm not asking you to do anything I wouldn't do. Just ask a few questions, visit the place a few times, and keep your eyes open."

"Okay. I can do that," I replied, relaxing.

Walters nodded. "Good. I'll see if we can get Michelle Thomson to go with you. She hasn't been out on the streets much yet. I doubt anyone would recognize her."

Michelle was also new and had been assigned to the Gang Suppression team. "Okay. Thanks."

Walters turned to the board behind him and began writing. "Let's shoot for Thursday. We'll have you two visit Griffin's from four to six. Two women going to Happy Hour. No drinking, of course."

"Maybe they should and just nurse them," said Fred. "Might be a little suspicious if one of them isn't drinking booze."

"He's right," I replied. "Especially a dive like that."

"By the way, how do you know when Happy Hour is, boss?" asked Bronson, smiling.

"Same way you should know. From surveillance. Know your enemy," said Walters. "Just like it's important to know the best times to order chicken wings, nachos, and deep fried mozzarella sticks."

"Their burgers are pretty good, too," said Fred.

"You too, huh?" said Bronson, chuckling. "I suppose you both know when the sexiest strippers are dancing, too?"

"None of them come out until after eight p.m. now," said Fred. "So, during the day, it's just a regular old bar and grill. The place has recently changed, probably because of Tank's Old Lady, Raina."

"Good to know," I said, relieved. At least during our reconnaissance I wouldn't have to stare at naked women bending over and gyrating in front of me.

"Speaking of burgers," said Walters. "You may as well use that as your excuse for trying the place out. Tell them you heard they were the best in town."

"Sure," I replied, already on it.

"And sit at the bar so you can strike up a conversation with the bartender," he added. "I think they might even have a couple of the bikers working as bartenders now."

"Perfect," I replied.

"Remember, be flirty but not too aggressive," he said. "And, dress a little like a biker chick, you know? Jeans and maybe something low-cut. Do you own any Harley T-shirts?"

"No. Afraid not," I replied, staring up at him.

"Just wear something that shows a little skin then. Not too much, though. You want to make it out of there in one piece."

"What about my hair?" I asked, a little aggravated. I was being treated like I didn't know what in the hell I was doing. "Should I wear it up like I am now, or look like I just got laid?"

Walters's eye twitched. He put his hands on the table and leaned toward me. "This is your first undercover job, correct?" he asked, staring at me hard.

I nodded.

40

"As much as you might think you know everything right now, Detective O'Brien, the fact is you don't know squat about these pieces of shit or what they're really capable of. One of them decides that you have something they like, you might be in the back room, down on your knees getting mouth-raped."

"And what makes you think I won't castrate the 'piece of shit' in the process?" I asked evenly.

He grunted. "Even with the barrel of a gun pointed at your temple?"

"Some things are worth dying for," I retorted, crossing my arms over my chest. "Especially my blow jobs, which are rare, numbered, and pretty goddamn priceless. No way in hell I'm giving those out for free."

Pen burst out laughing.

"Oh, hell," said Fred, shaking his head with a grin. "We got ourselves a firecracker."

"She's Irish and a redhead," said Bronson. "What'd you expect?"

"Really? You're going to stereotype?" I replied, looking at him over my shoulder. I really couldn't stand Bronson. He was a hair shy from having me file a sexual harassment claim against him. "I suppose I have a bunch of brothers who drink too much and are overprotective, too?"

"Damn right you do," interrupted Walters. "*Us.* We're all family here now, O' Brien. None of us like to admit it, but we drink too much and always tell it like

41

we see it. Sometimes we're wrong, but most of the time we're right. One thing is for certain, we're all on the same side, so relax."

"Does that mean I can borrow one of my brother's cars for this little operation on Thursday?" I asked. There was no way in hell I wanted to use my own vehicle.

"Don't worry about using your car. We'll loan you one from the department," he replied.

I sighed. "They have anything that won't get me tagged as a cop before I make it into the parking lot? Maybe even something classy?"

"Biker bitches aren't classy," said Pen. "Not the ones I've seen, at least."

"Bullshit. I've seen photos of them in the files. One of them had a white Mercedes convertible," I replied.

"You're not pretending to be an Old Lady," reminded Walters. "Or a biker chick."

"She's going to be noticed no matter what," said Pen. "And maybe that isn't a bad thing."

"He's right. Whatever the case may be, I should try and fit in," I replied.

"Flash them your tits, that will make you fit in with the rest of the skanks that usually hang around Griffin's," said Bronson.

"Maybe you should come with and flash them yours. They are much bigger than mine," I sneered.

Bronson gave me a dirty look.

Walters grunted. "I'm beginning to wonder if your balls are as big as your mouth, O'Brien. I guess we're going to soon find out."

"Why don't you ask Bronson? He copped a feel in the copy room the other day," I said nonchalantly.

Walters's eyebrows shot up. "What was that?'

"Oh Jesus. You're really going to bring that up again? It was an accident," said Bronson, rolling his eyes. "I told you that."

"Back up the bus. What happened in the copy room?" asked Walters loudly.

"Bronson's a little clumsy with his hands, apparently," I replied, remembering how he'd acted like he was helping me up the ladder to get more copy paper. The palm of his hand ended up on my girl parts.

"My hand slipped. It was an accident," explained Bronson.

"O'Brien, you sure everything is cool?" asked Walters, ignoring him.

I let out a ragged sigh. "I'm fine," I replied, still giving Bronson the stink eye. Little did he know, however, that I now carried a mini audio recorder with me at the office, hidden in my jacket. He tried anything else, and I'd record him. "He said it was an accident. I'll just have to go with that."

Bronson's face muscles relaxed.

"I hope so because if I find out there are any more 'accidents' like that, I'll have your badge. You hear me?" threatened Walters.

Bronson shoved the box of donuts away. "Yeah. I hear you. Sheesh… you know I'm happily married."

"Won't be too happy if Ethel gets wind of your clumsy mitts," said Pen, pulling out a vapor cigarette.

Bronson scowled.

Walters took out his cell phone, which was buzzing. "Okay, enough," he said, staring down at it. "O'Brien, keep reviewing the Gold Viper files so you know what kind of shitheads we're dealing with. Also, take a trip over to Dazzle in the next day or so."

"Dazzle? The jewelry store?" I asked, surprised.

"Yes. Raptor's Old lady, Adriana, works there part-time. Strike up a friendly conversation about some of the jewelry there, so that if you run into her at the bar, you'll have something to talk about," he replied.

"Oh. Okay," I replied.

"The rest of you, we need to see if we can try and track down this Judge character," said Walters.

"I'm telling you, there's nothing out there on him," said Bronson.

"That's bullshit. You just haven't turned over the right stones," he replied. "He might seem untouchable, but he's human. He's made a mistake somewhere. We just need to find it."

"Have you guys interviewed any ex-employees of Griffin's?" I asked. "Maybe they can give us something."

"Surprisingly, they have a slow turnaround at that dump. But, we did speak to a gal named Misty, about two years ago. She used to bartend there," said Pen. "She didn't give us anything substantial, though."

"Pay her another visit," said Walters. "It's been a while. She might be willing to talk now."

"It's a fucking waste of time, I'm telling you," said Bronson.

"Adjust your attitude, Bronson. You're already on my shit-list this morning," warned Walters.

Bronson's eye twitched. "I'm just saying, she was too frightened to talk last time we checked in with her."

"*Was.* She might not be anymore," he replied.

Bronson shrugged.

"What about Raptor's ex?" asked Walters. "Brandy? Maybe she'd be willing to cough up some information now that it's been a while."

"She split town a couple of years back," said Bronson. "She has family here, though. I'm sure we can locate her if you really think it's worth it."

"We don't have anything else going on, so why not?" said Walters. "Find her and press her again, too."

"Will do," said Pen, jotting down notes.

"I'm heading over to Sal's for lunch," said Walters. "See if he knows anything about The Judge."

"That's Raina's uncle, right?" I asked. "The one engaged to Tank?"

"Yep. Sal and I go way back. In fact, we went to high school together," he replied. "And were on the same football team."

"You think he knows anything?" I asked.

"I highly doubt it, but I'm not going to let that stop me from picking his brain. One thing I do know is that he has little respect for criminals and I'm sure he's not thrilled about Tank and Raina's engagement."

"Is it true that her brother is a new Prospect for the Gold Vipers?" I asked, remembering that I'd read it in the file.

"Yes, he is," said Walters, putting his jacket on. "Before that, he was with the Devil's Rangers. No wonder Sal drinks like he does."

"The move from Devil's Rangers to Gold Vipers must have gone over very well," I mused.

Walters headed toward the door. "I'm sure they were quite pissed. Anyway, let's see if we can get something useful in the next few days. We need to find out who killed Slammer and get our hands on the Judge."

"And I'd like to win the lottery," muttered Bronson as Walters walked out of the conference room.

Four

COLE

AFTER **FINISHING UP** with the garbage disposal, I ran into Tank and Raina again on my way out to lunch.

"Where you heading now?" Tank asked, his arm around my sister's shoulder.

"Was going to grab a bite to eat and check on Sal," I replied, twirling my keys around my finger. "Unless you need me for something right now."

"No, man. Go and get yourself some lunch. You've been working your ass off today."

"Thanks."

"I should go with you," said Raina. Sal, our uncle, had admitted himself into an alcohol rehabilitation center three weeks ago. He'd been diagnosed with liver disease and things weren't looking too good for him.

"Don't you have to get back to the bar?" I asked her. Both she and I were now co-owners of Sal's bar. Since I was already working two jobs, I wasn't able to help out much but Raina insisted that she could handle running the place.

"Yeah, but Matt's there. I'll just call him and tell him I'm going to be a little late," she replied.

Raina had promoted one of the bartenders to manager status. Even though he was a hard worker, this had pissed off some of the other waitresses, especially a woman named Marie, who'd given her a hard time even before the issue with Sal's health.

"Sounds good," I said, wanting to spend some time with Raina anyway. Both of us were always heading the opposite direction.

"How's he been doing?" asked Tank.

"Sal? I spoke to him last night and he said that he was beginning to handle things a little better. The first couple of weeks were hell, though," said Raina. "He went through withdrawals and had a pretty rough time. Hopefully the worst is over."

"Good to hear. I like that old fart. He needs to get better so he can walk you down the aisle," said Tank.

"That's what I keep telling him. Surprisingly, he likes you, too," said Raina.

"Princess, what's not to like?" he said puffing out his chest and grinning wickedly. "I'm not only good looking, I'm great with kids and have a soft spot for his niece. Plus, I can always help run Sal's if needed."

"I'm sure you could. Cole and I have it covered, though. In fact," she said, turning toward me, "I was hoping to start training you on a few things so that we could run the place together eventually. That way you wouldn't have to bounce at Griffin's."

I looked at Tank.

He shrugged. "She needs you more than I do. I can always hire new security."

"Exactly. You know, I've been putting in so many hours that I'm not spending as much time with Billy as I'd like."

"I'd like to see more of you, too," remarked Tank.

She leaned up and kissed him.

"Speaking of Billy, where is he now?" I asked. I missed my nephew and knew that if things didn't change soon, he wouldn't remember who I was.

"With Grandma Frannie," she replied.

Frannie was Tank's step-mom.

"Cool. Well, I have to work a few days at Griffin's, but I have Sunday off. Maybe we could start then?" I suggested.

"Jessica and Jordan are returning Sunday," said Tank. "I was hoping you could drive with me to the airport and pick them up. What about Friday? You can have that day off."

"You sure? You know how crazy it gets there Friday nights," I said. Especially when the strippers took the stage.

"Let me worry about that," said Tank. "Help Raina with Sal's and I'll figure something out. Hell, maybe I'll have Cheeks bounce," he said, smirking. "She's a tough bitch. In fact, tougher than most of the customers that walk through the front door."

Cheeks was one of the waitresses at Griffin's. She used to hang around the clubhouse and rumor had it that she'd slept with Tank a few times. Apparently now they were just friends. My sister didn't have a clue about their past, however. If she did, the woman would be waitressing somewhere else. I liked Cheeks, though, and it was obvious that she knew exactly where she stood now that Raina was Tank's Old Lady.

"I heard that she started dating your new cook, Levi," said Raina.

"Yeah, it looks that way. He's a nice guy," said Tank. "Not only does he make a hell of a burger, he's dependable. Never late and puts in extra hours."

"I guess we know why," said Raina, smiling.

"I guess we do," said Tank.

Raina looked at her watch. "We should get going. I need to pick up Billy soon."

"Yeah, and we have a meeting at two. Don't forget," said Tank.

"I won't," I replied, still wondering why I'd been invited.

He leaned over and kissed Raina goodbye, then my sister and I walked out the door.

"How's Billy doing?"

"Good," she said. "He asks about you all the time. You really need to stop by."

"I know. Maybe I'll stop by tomorrow and take him to the park."

"He'd love that," she replied.

I grinned. "Good. I'll check my work schedule and see what time I get off."

"Where you working tomorrow?"

"The auto body shop. Dou want a ride?" I asked, nodding toward my bike.

"No. I drove," she said, digging in her purse for her keys.

"Okay. I'm going to grab a sandwich really quick," I said, suddenly craving a Reuben. "Do you want me to pick you up anything? I'm heading over to Red's Deli."

"No, thank you. I brought Tank food already. We ate in his office."

"Okay. Meet you at the center in about forty minutes?"

"Sure," she said, getting into her car. "Drive safely."

"You, too," I replied, getting on my bike. I put my helmet and sunglasses on, then followed her out of the parking lot.

Five

TERIN

AFTER SPENDING THE next couple of hours going through files, I rubbed my temples and sat back in the chair.

"Fun stuff, huh?" remarked Fred, walking past me with a cup of coffee.

"A laugh a minute," I replied, smiling at him.

He nodded toward the clock. "You should take a break and grab a bite to eat."

"You know, that's a good idea," I answered, my stomach growling at the mention of food. Anyone want me to bring back lunch?"

Pen, whose desk was nearest to mine, asked where I was going.

"I don't know. I'm in the mood for a salad or maybe a sandwich," I replied.

"I know just the place," he said. "You should check out that deli on Fourth Street. They've got the best Philly cheesesteak sandwiches in town. They were featured on some food station show last summer, too."

"Red's Delicatessen?" I asked, recalling the place. I'd never been there but had heard the food was amazing.

"That's it. Here," he said, reaching into his wallet. He stood up and walked over to my desk. "You fly and I'll buy."

I waved my hand. "No. I'll certainly go, but you don't have to pay for my lunch."

"Nonsense. You can buy next time," he said, throwing a twenty dollar bill down in front of me. "Just get me one of those Phillies and a bag of pretzels. That's all I ask."

I picked the bill up. "Okay, thank you. Anyone else?"

"Could you bring back a piece of their blueberry pie?" asked Bronson. "I'll pay you when you get back."

"Sure." I turned to Fred, who was now sitting down at his desk. "Do you want anything?"

He held up a brown bag. "No. My wife actually made me a lunch today. Thanks, though."

"How is she doing?" I asked, knowing that his wife, Lilly, had recently lost her sister to lung cancer.

"Oh, she's doing all right," he replied, removing his eyeglasses. He began wiping them with a handkerchief. "She has her good days and bad ones. They were so close."

"They were twins, weren't they?" I asked.

He nodded. "Yes. It's been very difficult but... I'm hoping that when our granddaughter Shawna comes to stay with us during Christmas, she'll have something to smile about again."

"Shawna is in college, right?" I asked, knowing how much he loved talking about her.

"Yes," he replied, his face beaming. "She's studying to be a doctor."

"That's wonderful," I replied. "How many years of schooling does she have left?"

He chuckled. "Oh, about ten. She wants to be a brain surgeon."

"Wow. Ambitious girl," said Pen from the other side of me.

"Tell me about it. If anyone can do it she can. Smart as a whip and has the memory of an elephant," he said. "Unlike her grandfather. I have a hard time remembering what I ate this morning."

"Bullshit. You've got a great memory," said Pen. He looked at me. "Doesn't matter who he meets, this guy remembers first and last names, telephone numbers, and even eye colors. He's the go-to guy for details."

"Impressive," I replied, meaning it. "She must get it from you then."

"I reckon so," admitted Fred, smiling proudly. "But she definitely got her beauty and sweetness from Lilly and her mother, Priscilla."

"Come on now, I'm sure you made all the women swoon back in the day," I told him. I figured Fred to be in his late sixties now, but with his sparkling blue eyes and contagious smile, it was easy to see that he'd once been a very good looking guy.

He gave me a modest smile. "I held my own. That's for sure. Caught me a beauty, though. I suppose that says something."

"I think she caught you," I replied, winking. "Anyway, I'd better get going." I shoved the money into my purse and stood up. "I'll be back."

"Be careful. That's a bad area of town," said Fred, putting his eyeglasses back on.

I bit back a smile. "I think I can handle it."

"He's right; although, it's not so bad during lunchtime," said Pen. "Just stay out of the alley."

"You know I'm a cop, too, right? I carry a gun and even know how to use it," I said, winking.

"Sorry," said Pen, smiling. "You just remind me so much of my daughter. You even look a little like her."

"Who's your daughter?" asked Bronson. "Mila Kunis?"

"Mila Kunis? Who's that?" asked Pen.

"An actress. She was the dark-haired hottie in 'That 70s Show'. Jackie. O'Brien kind of looks like her, but with red hair. You ever think of dying it black?"

"Why would I want to do that?" I answered dryly.

"Black would look good on you. The color of your hair is almost too bright," he answered.

"Unlike you?" I muttered.

Bronson grunted. "You know what your problem is, you think you're so much better than everyone else."

"Not really," I said. "Just you."

Fred and Pen laughed.

A vein began to throb on his forehead. He opened his mouth to say something, but then changed his mind. "Dyke," he said under his breath as he turned away.

"What was that?" I asked sharply. I really didn't like this guy. *No wonder the only pie Bronson gets is the kind he has to pay for.*

Ignoring me, he began typing on his laptop.

"Don't listen to him," said Pen, scowling at Bronson's back. "He's just mad because you called him out earlier in front of Walters."

"Whatever," said Bronson over his shoulder. "I didn't do anything to O'Brien. Not on purpose, at least."

My eyes narrowed. "Yeah, just like you didn't call me a 'dyke'. By the way, my cousin is gay so you'd better watch your mouth or next time, I will report you."

"Maybe I should report you for annoying the fuck out of me," he said.

"You know, they say that excessive swearing is a weakness. It shows ones inability to speak intelligently or prove a valid point," I said.

"Maybe you should think about swearing more, since you're not making any valid points either," he retorted

"Ignore him," said Pen. "He's not worth your attention."

"That's for sure." I headed toward the door. "I'll be back."

"Thanks for the warning," said Bronson.

I gave him a dirty look.

He snorted. "I'm just giving you shit. You should learn to take a couple of jabs without blowing a fucking gasket. It's what we do here. Give each other crap from time to time. It relieves some of the stress we have to deal with."

"Seems like you're creating more than relieving it," I replied. "And this isn't my first rodeo. I've worked with other detectives before and there's a difference between giving each other shit and being downright insulting."

"Let me guess – it's your time of the month?" he replied.

I rolled my eyes. "You really are something special, aren't you? Your wife must love it when you're working overtime."

"Leave her alone," said Fred, when Bronson opened his mouth to retaliate. "Enough is enough."

"Oh, she's fine... right, O'Brien?" said Bronson, leaning back in his chair. He clasped his fingers over his pot belly. "Just like she said before... this isn't her first rodeo. And... if she's going to dish it out, she needs to learn how to take it, right?"

As far as I was concerned, I'd taken enough. "Sure. Whatever you say, Bronson," I said dryly. "I'll be back."

"Don't forget the pie," he said as I walked toward the doorway.

Resisting the urge to pull out my gun and shoot him in his pie-*hole*, I left the office.

***

Fifteen minutes later, I was in line at the deli, waiting for the cashier to ring up my order, when I noticed two men walk in. Both were dressed in Devil's Rangers cuts. Knowing that the deli was far from their Davenport clubhouse, I wondered what they were doing in Jensen. As good as the food probably was at Red's, I had an inkling that it wasn't the deli that had brought them into town.

"Pete here?" one of them asked as they stopped next to the register.

"He's in his office," said the cashier, looking uneasy.

"Tell him that Ronnie is here and I want to talk to him," he said, grabbing a mint from the candy dish next to the register. He was tall, thin, and had a dark Mohawk. There were pockmarks on his face and he had a small white scar near his lower lip. As he popped the mint into his mouth, I noticed he had the words "Fuck You" tattooed onto his knuckles.

"Uh, sure," she replied and then hurried away.

The other biker grabbed a mint too, and as he opened the wrapper, winked at me.

"Hey, sweet thing. How are you doing today?" he asked, smiling. He was bald and muscular, with yellow teeth, and plugs in his ears. He had a pot plant tattooed on one forearm and on the other, the Devil riding a horse. Underneath that were the words "Devil's Ranger."

"I'm doing fine," I said, noticing that he smelled like reefer and his pupils were dilated. "How about yourself?"

His eyes wandered past my gray blazer, over my matching wool skirt and to my black pumps.

"You certainly look like you're doing fine. You here alone?" he asked, grabbing another piece of candy.

Before I could answer, his buddy, Ronnie, laughed. "Really, Chips? Even if she is alone, a classy broad like her isn't going to give you the time of day, dumbass."

"Fuck you," said Chips. He turned back to look at me. "Sorry about my friend. He can be a real dickhead at times. Anyway, what's your name, darlin'?"

"Terin," I replied as someone else behind the deli counter handed me my order. I noticed that the young man, who was about eighteen, looked a little frightened. "Thank you."

He nodded and went back to help the next customer.

"Terin, huh? That's an interesting name. Looks like you have enough food there to feed an army," said Chips.

"Close. I've got some hungry coworkers who love to eat. So, your name is Chips?" I replied.

"That's my road name," he replied.

"Why that one?" I asked.

"I eat a lot of chips." He grinned and wiggled his eyebrows. "That being said, my lady friends like to call me 'Box'."

"Is that right?" I answered, rolling my eyes inwardly.

He laughed. "Sure is. So, you going to give me your number, or what?"

Before I could answer, the cashier returned.

Pete coming up here?" he asked.

I stared at the cashier's face, noticing that she looked even more anxious than before. She licked her lips and told them that Pete wasn't around.

"Bullshit. His car is parked in back," said Ronnie, raising his voice.

"Really? Maybe he went for a walk." The cashier looked at me. "Your total comes to twenty-nine dollars and fifteen cents," she said, ringing me up.

"Okay." I handed her my credit card. Her hand shook as she swiped it in the machine.

"Went for walk. Right," said Ronnie, nodding to Chips. "Let's go find the fucker."

They both walked around the cashier and headed toward the back office.

"Shit," she said, looking frightened.

"What do they want with Pete?" I asked her.

The cashier began biting her nails. "I don't know."

"Was he back there?"

She didn't reply.

Sighing, I pulled out my badge. "Is he in trouble with those guys? If he is, you'd better say something. I can help."

She hesitated and then confessed. Lowering her voice, she said, "I think so. He slipped out the back when he heard they were here looking for him."

I was surprised that she'd been courageous enough to lie to the two bikers. I looked around the dining area. Fortunately, there were only a couple of people eating. Some of the other patrons had left when the two bikers had entered the place. "Okay. Just to be on the safe side, tell the rest of the staff and customers to leave."

Two people who were waiting in line and listening, didn't even hesitate. They anxiously headed for the front door, not looking back. The cashier spoke to her coworkers and then made her way to the dining room while I crept down the hallway to see what was happening with Pete.

"See, that piece of shit was here. The coffee is still hot," said Chips angrily. "Look, there's back door. He probably ran out that way. Let's go and get our money."

Warning bells went off in my head. If Pete owed them money, the situation was just as dangerous as I'd assumed. I knew I should call for backup, but every moment wasted could prove more dangerous for Pete. The Devil's Rangers were violent and I knew that if the deli owner was trying to run from them, he probably didn't have their money. I opened up my jacket and unclipped my Glock from the holster.

"Should I get out of here?" whispered the cashier, now standing next to me.

"Yeah. Do me a favor and call the police."

Nodding, she turned around and disappeared.

Holding my gun, I entered the empty office and found the doorway Chips and Ronnie had exited. Peeking outside, I noticed the bikers surrounding a sedan. Ronnie had his gun pointed at the man in the driver's seat and motioned for him to get out of the car.

Pete rolled down the window. "I've got your money but it's in the bank!" he cried, looking frightened. "I was just going to withdraw what I owed you."

"You said that yesterday and never showed up at the clubhouse," said Ronnie, moving closer to the car.

Pete laughed nervously. "I know you're not going to believe this, but I ended up getting a flat tire. Once I got to the bank, it was closed and I could only withdraw three hundred dollars from the ATM. I knew you wanted it all, and was afraid that you'd be pissed. That's why I didn't show up last night. I was going to bring you the entire amount today though. I swear to God."

"Always an excuse," said Ronnie.

"It's the truth," said Pete.

"Let's get in the car with him," Ronnie said to Chips. "We'll take a ride with ol' Pete here and make sure he doesn't have any more car trouble along the way."

"Yeah. Sure. You guys can ride down with me. Just so you know, though, I might not have the entire amount," said Pete. "But, I have most of it."

"You were supposed to have the entire amount yesterday. You know what happens when we don't get what's owed to us, don't you?" threatened Ronnie.

"I'll have the rest by Friday. I swear," said Pete, his voice cracking.

"Friday will be too late. Get in the fucking car, Chips," ordered Ronnie.

"What about Gomer?" asked Chips. "We should tell him we're leaving."

"Police! Put your gun down!" I ordered, stepping outside.

65

Ronnie turned and aimed the gun toward me.

"Drop your gun!" I hollered, grateful that the private parking lot was small and deserted. Behind that was an alleyway and a mini mall that wasn't being used for anything at the moment.

"You drop yours," he answered, cocking his.

"You're a fucking cop?" called out Chips, staring at me in shock.

"Yes, and if you don't put your gun down, Ronnie, you're going to jail," I said calmly.

"Mind your own business, pig," said Ronnie, his gun still raised. "This has nothing to do with you."

"It does now. Lower your weapon," I said firmly.

A smile spread across his face and someone grabbed me from behind, snatching my gun in the process. Furious, I elbowed the person as hard as I could. I heard a grunt and the man released me, but not before I elbowed him a second time and knocked the gun out of his hand.

"Dammit, Gomer!" groaned Ronnie. "You really are a pussy."

I quickly scrambled toward my Glock and was about to pick it up when Chips grabbed me around the waist and spun me away.

"Whoa, darlin'," he laughed and pulled me against his chest. "You're not having a lot of luck today, are you?"

"Let me go!"

66

I struggled to break free, but his arm was like a steel vice, holding me still.

"You're a little firecracker," said Chips, enjoying himself. "That's for sure."

Angry, I did a reverse head-butt, hitting Chips in the jaw, which hurt like hell. He grunted in pain, but instead of releasing me, he pulled out a knife.

"Don't move or I'll slit your throat," he snarled, his fingers wrapping around my bun.

I froze. "Fine," I muttered, feeling the tip of the knife against my throat. I raised my hands up slowly. "I'm not moving."

"Good girl," he said.

"It would be wise for you to let me go," I said, my teeth clenched.

"Why should I?" he said, pulling my head back roughly. "You're worth more to us dead."

"Exactly. We need to get rid of her," said Ronnie. "We can't have any witnesses. Especially a cop."

"I know," said Chips breathing heavily near my ear. "I'll take care of her."

"You sure you can handle her?" asked Ronnie, who'd been watching quietly with his gun poised on Pete.

"I can handle this little fox," said Chips, sniffing my neck. "Mm… what fragrance is that?"

"It's called Fuck Off," I muttered in revulsion as he began groping me.

Chips chuckled. "Feisty. I like that."

"Quit thinking with your pecker and handle this situation," ordered Ronnie, getting into Pete's car. "I'll meet you back at the clubhouse. Gomer, you stay with him and clean this shit up."

"Will do," said Gomer.

"Now... drive, before I kill you, dumb-shit," ordered Ronnie to Pete.

"What are you going to do with that young woman?" asked Pete, staring at us with wide eyes.

"Nothing you need to worry about," said Ronnie. "Just get me my money."

"I'm sorry, miss," said Pete, looking ashamed. "This situation is my fault."

"Drive!" ordered Ronnie, now holding the gun against the back of Pete's skull.

Pete put the car in gear and they took off down the alley.

"Please. Chips. Just... let me go," I said in a calm voice. "We can forget about all of this."

"Too late. We don't forget and we don't negotiate. Stupid nosy broad. You should have taken your food and gotten the fuck out of here," he replied angrily.

The alley was quiet and I began to wonder if the cashier had even bothered to call the cops.

"You're right. I should have minded my own business. But I still can, you know?" I told him. "We can all just go on our own way and forget we ever met."

He snorted. "I don't believe that for a second."

"We gotta do something with her," said Gomer, looking around the alley anxiously.

"I know," he replied. "Let me think."

It was then that I realized Chips was still attracted to me. I could feel his hardness push against my backside. As disgusting as it was, it gave me an idea. "Hey. Maybe we could work something out."

He grunted. "Like what?"

"Like... whatever you'd like," I said in a softer voice. I pressed against his crotch.

"What are you doing?" he asked.

"I'm not like most cops you've probably met," I said, wondering if death would actually be better than flirting with the disgusting pile of shit. "I know when to keep my mouth shut and I know how to make deals."

"What kind of deal are we talking about?"

"You get what you want and I forget I ever saw you," I whispered.

"What did she say?" asked Gomer, frowning.

"Nothing," said Chips, pulling me back a few steps. He lowered his voice. "Why should I believe that you'd keep your word?"

"Because, I'd rather not admit to my fellow cops that I traded sex for my life. I'd be the laughing stock of

69

the department. Plus, I'd have to go to court and," I laughed coldly, "what a drag that would be."

Chips was silent for a few seconds. "Gomer, check the deli. Make sure there aren't any customers and then lock the doors."

Holy crap. He's actually falling for it?

"On it," said Gomer, disappearing.

"Looks like we're going to have some private time together, darlin'," chuckled Chips, grinding his pelvis into my butt cheeks. "I'm not really stupid enough to believe that you wouldn't rat me out one way or another. Plus, Ronnie would kill me if I let you go. But, I'm still going to have my way with you. At least one of us will be having fun."

"Fuck you," I replied, swearing to myself that the only fun to be had would be hurting the son of a bitch.

He laughed. "That's the plan."

Six

COLE

THERE WAS ROAD construction on the same block as Red's Deli, which appeared to be hurting the business in the area. The shop itself was empty when I walked inside, even though the OPEN sign was lit up and three motorcycles were parked outside.

I took off my sunglasses. "Hello?" I called out, looking over the tall glass deli case.

Nothing.

Strange, I thought.

The lights were on, music played, and uneaten sandwiches sat on some of the tables. It was then that I heard the sound of the back door being opened and footsteps. I peered around the corner and swore inwardly when I noticed who was heading this way.

Gomer.

I should have recognized his Hog out front, I thought, heading back toward the front door. The last thing I needed at the moment was a confrontation with my old club. I knew the Devil's Rangers were beyond pissed that I'd switched teams, but I wasn't exactly happy with them either. Ronnie, the V.P., had made me believe that the Gold Vipers had orchestrated the drive-by shooting, which had almost killed Billy. When I'd first confronted Ronnie about it, he'd played stupid, but eventually confessed.

"Fuck the Gold Vipers," he'd said. "Slammer deserved to die and I'm glad it worked out the way it did. Even better, they can't pin his murder on any of us."

"What about my sister?" I'd replied angrily. "Not only is her life in danger now, but she could go to jail. Hell, we both could end up in prison if they find any evidence."

"Fuck that. You're being paranoid. The Vipers don't know who killed him and neither do the cops. Anyway, her finger had been itching to kill someone. Why not the person who deserved it more than anyone?"

"Because it wasn't right and you know it."

"The man was a murderer. He may have not been involved in what happened that night, but he fucking had it coming. Look at the trail of bodies he's left behind in the past couple of years. All Devil's Rangers. As far as I'm concerned, his death was long overdue."

"Not by Raina's gun."

"Jesus, give it a rest. You're acting like we set her up," he'd replied angrily.

"Didn't you?"

"How were we supposed to know that your sister was crazy enough to go after someone like him? You?" He'd smirked. "Of course, I must admit, the thought had crossed my mind. Hell I figured that if you did manage to kill the sonofabitch, I'd patch you, from Prospect to an actual club member, the very next day." He'd laughed. "Looks like your bad-assed sister beat you to it."

Those words had set me off. Not only did I beat the shit out of Ronnie that night, but I'd thrown my cut into the trash bin out back. It was the last conversation we'd had together.

"What the fuck are you doing here?" asked Gomer, noticing me trying to leave.

I turned around. At least he didn't have his gun pulled out.

"I'm just leaving," I said.

Gomer glared at me. "Good. Get the fuck out of here."

I heard the back door open again and a woman's voice, asking to be let go.

"What's going on?" I asked, tensing up.

"None of your business. Get out of here," said Gomer.

"Someone else here?" called Chips.

"Yeah," said Gomer, sighing.

"You'd better let me go. My entire department is going to be down here soon, wondering why they haven't gotten their food yet," a woman said angrily.

"Who's that?" I asked.

"Are you fucking kidding me?" barked Chips, dragging some chick around the corner. "Cole? What the fuck are you doing here?"

Realizing that I'd walked into a very bad situation, I lied. "Looking for Ronnie," I said, staring at the young woman dressed in business attire. She had dark red hair that was pulled back into a bun, and light green eyes that reminded me of Jade, Patty's cat. Oddly enough, the woman looked more pissed off than frightened.

"He just left. What do you need him for?" asked Chips, glaring at me with hatred.

"Some business between us," I replied.

Chips scowled. "Why would he want to do business with a fucking traitor?"

Although I now despised the Devil's Rangers, being called a traitor still made me feel like an asshole. "It's private shit. Between us."

While he stared at me with suspicion, the chick also watched me, a curious look in her eyes.

"Hey, did you lock that door yet, Gomer?" asked Chips.

"Shit. No. I'll do it now," he replied.

Chips shook his head. "Dumbass," he muttered.

I moved out of Gomer's way. He locked the door and turned the sign off.

"Who's the chick?" I asked casually, crossing my arms so I could get closer to my gun.

"My new friend," said Chips with a menacing grin. "Aren't you, doll?"

"I'm a cop and these two are going to jail," said the woman in an authoritative voice.

"Jail, huh?" Chips barked out a laugh. "Can you believe this broad? She just doesn't give up."

Gomer snorted. "She obviously doesn't understand the seriousness of the situation she's in."

"Sorry, little fox," said Chips. He licked the side of her face and she shuddered in horror. "Nobody is going anywhere. Not until we take care of business."

"Ronnie know what you're doing right now?" I asked.

"Hell yeah. He's the one who told us to take care of her, which is what we're planning on doing," said Gomer. "If you keep your mouth shut, we might let you have a piece, too."

"Bullshit. He's a fucking traitor. He's not getting anything," snapped Chips. "Unless it's a good ass kicking, which is a lot less than what he deserves."

"Where is Pete? The owner of this place?" I asked, ignoring him. One thing I knew about the man, other than his staff made excellent sandwiches, was that he was always working.

"Pete is with Ronnie," said Chips. "Making a pit stop at the bank."

"And what about the rest of the employees?" I asked.

"I don't know where they went," said Chips, glancing around the dining room. "They must have decided to cut early for the day."

"I sent them away," said the woman. "And told the cashier to call the cops."

"She obviously didn't. They'd be here by now," said Gomer as he stepped back around me.

I quickly pulled out my pistol and grabbed him by the collar. "Don't move or I'll put a bullet through your head," I said, shoving the gun against his temple.

Gomer raised his hands in the air. "I'm not moving. Relax."

"What the fuck you doing?" hollered Chips, glaring at me.

"Let her go," I ordered.

"Why? This bitch is a cop. Why do you care what happens to her?" asked Chips.

I ignored his question. "Do it, or I'll pull the fucking trigger," I said sharply. "Gomer's brains will be all over this place. I'm sure Bogie will love to hear how you chose a piece of tail over a brother. Especially *his*."

Bogie was Gomer's older brother. He was also the most unstable member of the Devil's Rangers. He'd once killed a UPS driver after the guy had stepped on his freshly seeded lawn. He'd also threatened a neighbor, whose Cottonwood trees had sent seeds over to his property. The man had been so terrified that he'd spent thousands of dollars to have them all cut down. To say that Bogie was a crazy fucker was an understatement. One thing for certain, however, he loved his younger brother Gomer and would kill Chips if anything happened to him.

Staring at me with hatred, Chips lowered the knife and pushed her away.

"Now, you'd better let him go if you know what's good for you," said Chips.

Before I could do anything, however, the angry chick straightened out her jacket and turned around. "Put the knife down."

He grunted at her. "Whatever."

"I'm only going to ask you one more time..." she said coldly.

"Fuck you, bitch," he answered. "Scram!"

Her eyes narrowed.

Chips grinned darkly. "Unless you really do want me to fuck you."

I could tell that comment made her even angrier. I was about to tell her to get lost when all of a sudden, she cried out in rage and then performed a roundhouse kick, her shoe connecting with his chin so hard, that even I could feel it in my jaw. Grunting in pain, Chips fell backward, dropping the knife.

She quickly picked it up and pointed it down at him. "Get your ass off of the floor. Now!" she ordered.

Chips spit out blood. "Fuck you, bitch!" he growled, crawling backward.

"Fine. Stay down there, asshole." She reached into her blazer and pulled out her cell phone. She dialed 9-1-1 and told them that she was an officer and needed assistance. Then she gave the operator the address.

Still glaring at the cop, Chips stood up and then looked at me. "Enough is enough. Let him go so we can all get the fuck out of here."

The woman took a step toward me. "Don't you dare. In fact," she held out her hand. "Give me your gun."

"Sorry. No can do," I told her.

Mumbling to herself, the woman pulled out her badge. "My name is Detective Terin O'Brien and I'm with the Jensen City Police Department. Give me your weapon."

"Fuck this," said Chips. He turned, ran down the hall, and out of the back of the deli.

"Dammit! Don't you dare let that one go!" she ordered, running off after him.

"You're not really going to turn me in, are you?" asked Gomer angrily.

"Maybe I should. I mean, you *were* going to rape her," I said. "That's pretty fucked up."

"What are you, some kind of saint now?" he asked with disgust.

"I'm certainly not a rapist but that doesn't make me a fucking saint either."

The sound of sirens in the distance made both of us swear.

"Get the fuck out of here," I said, releasing him.

"Wise choice," said Gomer before racing out the front door.

"That remains to be seen," I mumbled, slipping the gun back into my leather jacket. I thought about checking on Terin but decided she was probably doing fine on her own. Plus, I didn't feel like spending the rest of my afternoon filling out a police report.

Putting on my sunglasses, I rushed out of the deli, hopped onto my bike, and took off.

Seven

TERIN

I **QUICKLY FOLLOWED** Chips out of the building.

"Freeze!" I yelled, wishing I still had my gun.

Ignoring me, he kept running.

I tried chasing him down the alley, but unfortunately, my early morning shoe choice and the fact that his legs were much longer than mine, made it impossible to catch up. Out of breath, I stopped and walked back to the deli, both my feet and my ego sore. I just knew the fact that I'd blundered the arrest and lost my gun was going to make me the laughing stock of the office. I'd never hear the end of it, especially since I was a woman. The only thing I had going for me was that I could easily ID the three men from the Devil's Rangers and I wouldn't rest until I had Chips, Gomer, and Ronnie in handcuffs.

By the time I returned to the deli, backup had arrived but both the stranger and Gomer were gone. I reported what happened to the other officers on the scene and a few minutes later, two familiar faces walked in. Walters and Bronson.

Bronson smirked. "What's going on O'Brien? You scare everyone out of the place?"

I explained what had happened.

"Devil's Rangers, huh?" said Walters. He looked at Bronson. "Let's put out an APB for those three assholes."

"Okay," he replied, making notes.

Walters turned back to me. "So, Ronnie left with Pete. What was the make and model of his vehicle?"

"It was a newer white Toyota Camry. I memorized the license plate," I said, giving it to him.

"Good. What about the other guy? You know who he was?" asked Walters.

"I think it might have been Cole Johnson," I replied, remembering the conversation. "Chips mentioned that he'd screwed them over."

"I'm sure a lot of people have screwed those dirtbags over, and vice-versa. Was he wearing a cut?" he asked.

I sighed. "I couldn't tell. He had on a black leather jacket. No patches."

"What did he look like?"

The word 'handsome' popped into my head and almost escaped my lips. "He, um, he was about six foot two, black hair cropped, blue eyes, darker complexion... possibly Italian or Greek decent," I replied.

"Any tattoos or piercings noticeable?"

"Nothing on his face. No piercings that I could see. Like I said, he was wearing a jacket."

"Your description sounds like it could be him," said Pen, who had just walked into the deli and was now standing next to us.

"It does, although we can't know for sure until O'Brien IDs him," agreed Walters. "We'll round him up too and get a statement. Let's pay a little visit to the Gold Vipers' clubhouse."

"You want me with?" I asked. "Make sure it's the right guy?"

He sighed. "You may as well. I doubt we can have you going undercover now anyway. If it wasn't Cole, it's going to be someone who associates with one of the clubs."

"True. Sorry," I replied.

"It's not your fault, O'Brien. You were just in the wrong place at the wrong time," he replied.

"Or… maybe she was in the right place at the right time, especially if Pete ends up dead," said Pen.

"Old Pete's lucky," he answered. "Once Ronnie finds out you're still alive, they're going to let him go. Money or not."

I nodded.

Walter's phone rang. When he answered it, Pen asked how I was doing.

"Much better if I hadn't made such a rookie move," I replied, smiling grimly. "I should have called for backup right away."

He shrugged. "Probably. At least you walked out of the situation alive. Normally they don't leave witnesses."

"And they wouldn't have, if not for Cole," I said. "I'm surprised he did what he did and helped me."

"Don't be. Cole Johnson has a sister, and from what I hear, a soft spot for women," he replied. "Especially pretty ones."

I smiled. "Even so, he's still a member of the Gold Vipers and from the files I've been reading, they are not exactly altar boys."

He chuckled. "That's true. These guys are dangerous and think they're above the law. Slammer certainly did and I'm sure as hell Tank feels the same way. When it comes to women and children, however, they won't hesitate to lend a helping hand. Even when the one needing assistance isn't part of their club family."

"Like modern day Robin Hoods, in other words?" I asked, amused. "Helping damsels in distress and stealing from the rich... only filling their pockets instead of the poor's?"

"That's probably how some of them see it," he replied.

"Is that what they told you?" I asked.

"No. My niece did, and believe me, she knows them pretty well."

I stared at him in confusion. "Your niece?"

He nodded and sighed. "My sister's kid. Yes. We don't speak much anymore, but she knows most of them pretty well."

Something about the expression on his face told me that he was less than thrilled about the idea.

"So, how does she know them?"

"She's basically a Gold Viper roadie," he said with a sour expression.

The term "club whore" came to my mind. "Oh."

"You'll probably meet her eventually. She goes by the name of Cheeks. She also bartends at Griffin's."

"Oh," I repeated, not exactly sure how to respond.

"Her real name is Maddy. My sister died when Maddy was eighteen and she started hanging out with some of the club members. Eventually, she got to be really good friends with Tank and Raptor."

"Hmm… What did she tell you about them?"

"Not much. She mentioned that they always treated her with respect and she felt at home with them." He smiled humorlessly. "I tell you one thing, though, my sister Julia must have turned over in her grave when Maddy hooked up with that lot. Julia was a good, church-going woman. Very strict, though. Maybe even too strict at times. Maddy was very sheltered and wasn't even allowed to date. Probably why she went so man-crazy after her mother died. Decided to sow her oats and make up for lost time."

"You said she's happy though?"

"Yeah. As far as I know, she's not into drugs and has been dating a new guy, who isn't a Gold Viper. I guess that's something."

I nodded.

Walters walked back over to us, a thoughtful expression on his face. "The department just received an anonymous tip in regards to the vehicle used during Slammer's shooting."

Up until now, the only thing we knew was that it was green, an older model van, and possibly a Chevy. Two women had noticed it parked and idling across the street from the credit union, near the time of the shooting. They'd also witnessed a young woman wearing a hoodie and dark sunglasses entering the bank. Unfortunately, the video footage shot inside of the building hadn't given many details on the assailant, other than it was definitely a petite female with possibly brown or black hair.

"So, what did you find out?" I asked

"Get ready for a shocker... Someone called, about ten minutes ago, claiming that the shooter was Raina Davis, and the driver of the van was her brother, Cole Johnson."

Eight

COLE

I **DROVE BACK** to the clubhouse and called Raina to let her know that I wouldn't be able to meet her.

"Why?"

"Some club business."

She let out a frustrated sigh.

"Sorry, Raina. Tell Uncle Sal that I'll visit him tomorrow."

"What kind of club business, Cole?"

"Nothing you need to worry about," I replied, knowing that Tank wouldn't want me telling anyone anything. Least of all Raina. If he wanted her to know, he'd do it himself later. After I told him.

"Cole–"

"I gotta go," I said, walking back toward Tank's office. "Bye."

I hung up before she could grill me anymore. Now that Raina was engaged to Tank, she was always trying to pry info from me. It was because she knew so little that I knew opening my big mouth would have been a mistake.

I knocked on Tank's door.

"Come in," he said.

When I entered his office, Tank was alone and staring at his laptop, wearing eyeglasses.

"I didn't know you wore cheaters," I said, sitting down in front of him.

He took them off and shoved them into his desk. "Only once in a while."

"You see an eye doctor?" I asked.

"No. I'm sure it's because I haven't been getting a lot of sleep. What's up?" he asked. "I thought you were on your way to see Sal?"

I told him what had happened at the deli.

"Good. They're royally fucked now," he replied, smiling.

I nodded. "Hopefully I'm not in too much trouble. She wanted me to stick around, but I hauled my ass out of there when I heard the sirens."

He leaned back in his chair and sighed. "The cops will be showing up here. They'll want to talk to you."

"They couldn't see my cut," I replied, unzipping my leather jacket. "So, I doubt the woman even knew who I was."

"Did either of those two idiots mention your name?"

I thought back. "I don't think so."

"Not that it's a big deal. I've got nothing to hide. I just don't like them coming into my clubhouse and snooping around." He chewed on his lower lip. "Actually, why don't you just go to them? They could use you to back up her story."

I stared at him in surprise.

"Normally, I wouldn't suggest it, but those dirt-bags have it coming," he explained.

"Okay. If that's what you want. I'll leave right now," I said, wondering if he was testing my loyalty to the club somehow.

"Good idea. Get it over with. And Ice, don't let them coerce you into giving any kind of intel on *us*."

"I'd never do that," I said, a little hurt that he felt he needed to remind me. "Seriously, I want you to know that I'm committed to the club. In fact, I swear on my life, I'd *never* double-cross you."

Tank smiled. "I believe you, brother, and I'm not worried that you'd do anything on purpose. I just know that once you're downtown and getting grilled, they'll try to put words into your mouth. Don't let them."

"I won't," I said firmly.

"Speaking of heat, what did you say her name was?"

"Terin O'Brien. Tell you one thing – she sure didn't look like a cop," I replied, thinking she was hotter than any I'd ever seen.

"What do you mean?"

"Let's just say that if you saw her, you'd want to be frisked. She did a number on Chips, though. Kicked him in the chin and he went down hard. It was pretty comical."

Tank grunted. "Sounds like he got what he deserved. I wonder if she caught the fucker."

"From the amount of sirens headed toward the deli, I'm sure someone got a hold of him."

"Chips is a piece of shit," said Tank, staring ahead. "He's been to Griffin's a few times. Once we had to kick him out because he started touching some of the girls and wouldn't stop."

"No surprise there," I replied.

"Swear to God, the Devil's Rangers must recruit their members directly from the neighborhood sex offender list. They're all fucking deviants." Tank's smile fell and he gave me an apologetic look. "Shit. No offense."

I chuckled. "None taken. Even I have to admit, most of them are fuck-nuts."

"Lucky you left."

"No shit. Unlucky I ever got involved with them. Worst thing I ever did."

He shrugged. "You didn't know what those guys were about."

"Actually, I kind of did," I said, feeling shitty. "I mean, I didn't know everything. I just knew that they were one-percenters and I liked the sound of it."

"Let me tell you something – obviously, you can be a one-percenter and not be a degenerate. That's the problem with those fuckers. They have no integrity and play dirty with other clubs. They're nothing but pieces of shit and I hope that eventually, they'll just fade away all together."

"There aren't too many chapters left," I replied. "Maybe three?"

"That's what I heard too. Anyway, their time is coming. After this, maybe even faster than we think."

I nodded.

Tank looked at his watch. "You should get down to the station soon. I have a feeling you're going to be there for a while."

"What about church?" I said, checking the time.

"Looks like you're going to miss it. There's always next week."

"Why was I invited?" I asked bluntly.

"What do you mean?"

"I'm a Prospect. Normally we're not asked to be there for the weekly ones."

He smiled. "Honestly, I wanted you to go over what you knew about the Devil's Rangers. Not just who's who, but what kind of deals they were working on and who they might have double-crossed lately."

I nodded. "Sure. I can do that. They've made enemies, that's for sure."

"One of those enemies almost killed your nephew. I'd like to find out who."

"Me, too. Believe me, I've been racking my brain trying to figure out who they were."

"They rode in on motorcycles?"

"Yeah. Sounded like Harleys."

"You couldn't identify them by patches?"

"To be honest, I wasn't around when it happened. I was taking a leak. I heard the commotion but didn't see anything."

"Why did you assume they were us?" he asked.

"Just like I said before, Ronnie told me. I had no reason to doubt him back then. And the way they talked about you and the club, it just seemed logical."

"Hell, I could hear the praises now," he said with a smirk. "What about your ex? Patty? She must have seen the shooters."

"After I found out that you weren't the ones behind the attack, I tried talking to her about it but she couldn't remember much. Just that they were bikers and looked scary."

"She wouldn't recognize any of them?"

I shrugged. "I don't know. To be honest, we got into this huge fight afterward and I haven't seen her since." She'd actually wanted to get back with me but I'd lost all respect and feelings for Patty. It wasn't that I hated her for what she'd done by showing up with my nephew at that party, which I probably should have. I pitied the fact that she was so insecure, especially since I'd never given her reason to be.

"Maybe I should talk to her," said Tank, grabbing a piece of paper.

"You sure you want to do that?" I asked.

"If it will help find out who those assholes were, of course. Don't worry, I'm not going to hurt her."

"I wasn't worried about her, I was worried about you," I joked. "She can be very stubborn and temperamental."

He grinned. "Most women are. What's her address?"

I gave it to him.

He wrote it down. "Where does she work?"

"Last I heard, she was waitressing at Rumors."

"Okay. Good to know."

"Do you want me to go with you?"

Crossing his arms over his chest, he leaned back in the chair again. "No," he said, staring off. "Something tells me it's a bad idea. If Patty is still mad at you, she might be too pissed off to cooperate. I'll bring Tail with me. He has a way of making women talk."

"She's a head-case, so tell him not to fuck her or she'll be looking at wedding rings the next morning."

He grinned. "Noted."

Nine

TERIN

"**R**AINA? **SHE AND TANK** are engaged, aren't they?" I asked, stunned.

"Yes," Walters replied. "I'm sure it's bullshit. The Devil's Rangers are trying to pin this on them because of what happened today. And then there's the other obvious reason - Cole deserted the club and is now with the Gold Vipers. That must have really charred them."

"The guys here tonight were definitely pissed off at him," I replied. "The man, if it really was Cole, did mention that he was supposed to meet with Ronnie, their V.P. I wonder what that was all about?"

He frowned. "Hmm… not sure and I doubt we'll ever find out."

"Do you think it might be possible that Cole is spying on the Gold Vipers for Ronnie?"

He scratched his head and smiled grimly. "With these guys, anything is possible. Questioning him about Slammer's murder is sounding better by the moment."

"What about Cole's sister? Maybe we should talk to her as well?"

"Raina? She's marrying Slammer's son. He'd be putting a bullet through her heart instead of a ring around her finger."

"What if he didn't know she did it?"

He gave me a curious look.

"Better yet, what if he *did* know?" I said, the idea making the hair stand up on the back of my neck. "What if it was a setup and Tank wanted his old man killed so that he could become president or maybe something else was going on between them?"

"It's a good theory if you didn't know how tight they were. Tank looked up to his old man and when he learned about his death, my sources say he took it very hard."

"What about Slammer's new wife?" I asked, having read that he'd remarried a couple of years before. "Maybe she needed money and decided to cash out on his insurance policy?"

"We already checked that out. In fact, I personally interviewed her after he was murdered and she seemed pretty upset. The insurance policy was big but not substantial. Most of it went to his son, Tank, anyway."

"Did you get a chance to talk to Cole and Raina's uncle, Sal?" I asked.

"No. I learned that he's in some kind of a rehab center right now."

"Drugs?"

"I doubt it. He always was a drinker, though. Probably for that." Walters's phone began to ring again. "Excuse me," he said, answering it. Shock registered across his face as the person on the other end spoke.

"Thanks. We'll be down shortly," he said, hanging up.

"What's going on?" I asked.

"That was Bronson. Apparently, Cole Johnson just showed up at the station. He wants to give a statement about what happened today at Red's Deli."

I stared at him in disbelief. "You're kidding? I thought we were going to have to drag him down there, especially after the way he took off."

"This is definitely a new one for me. Normally these guys refuse to work with us."

"Maybe Cole found out that someone is trying to frame him and his sister for Slammer's murder?"

He shoved his phone back into his pocket. "That's entirely possible. I guess we'll find out soon enough."

Something in my gut told me that even though we'd be interviewing him, and voluntarily, the answers we received wouldn't exactly be the ones we needed.

Ten

COLE

A S I WAITED to speak with Detective O'Brien, I sat alone in one of the interrogation rooms, drinking coffee and playing games on my phone. It was then that I received a text from Patty. Groaning inwardly, I read her message.

Some guy named Tank called and left a message for me about the shooting. Isn't he the leader of the Devil's Rangers?

Me: *No. He's the president of the Gold Vipers, the club I'm now with.*

Patty: *What does he want with me?!*

Me: *He just wants to talk to you about that night. See if you remember anything useful about the shooters.*

She called me and I reluctantly picked it up.

"Dammit, Cole! Why did you give him my phone number?"

"Because he asked for it."

"Well, I'm not talking to him and I'll call the cops if he shows up at my job or my home."

"No, you won't," I replied as calmly as I could. "You'll answer his questions truthfully and be courteous."

"Quit telling me what to do," she snapped. "I don't have to do anything I don't want to."

"Not even for Billy?"

She gasped. "Look, I told you how sorry I was for what happened and..." there were tears in her voice, "he's fine now. Billy is fine and I thank God for that every night."

"So do we."

I could hear her blowing her nose on the other end of the phone. "Sorry," she said after a few seconds. "I still lose it when I think about that night. I keep reliving it in my head, over and over."

"And you don't remember anything about the guys on the motorcycles?"

"Not really." She started crying again. "Dammit, Cole, why can't you just let things rest so we can all move forward?"

I lowered my voice. "Because we need to know who did it."

"Well... I don't know!" she cried.

"Calm down," I said, softening my voice.

"I will if you quit drilling me about that night. I've told you so many times now, I don't know who in the hell they were. All I heard were the shots and I only caught a glimpse of the drivers. Honestly, I couldn't tell the difference between one club and another."

"What about their patches?"

"I told you I couldn't see any patches," she said. "Why do you keep asking me the same things over and over? Do you have any idea how upsetting this is?"

"I'm sorry this is upsetting you," I said, trying not to lose my cool. "Think about how upset Raina was when she found out about Billy. She almost lost everything that night."

"I know and I'm sorry," she said sadly. "I did something so stupid, and believe me, if I could go back in time and change things, I would. I'm just glad that he's alive."

"So are we. Still, don't you think the men responsible for hurting him should pay?"

"You mean go to jail?" she asked dryly. "Or pay with blood?"

I wanted to ask her why she even cared. She could have died that night. "Patty, if you won't talk to him for me, at least do it for Raina and Billy. See if the two of you can come up with something," I said, ignoring her snide comment.

"All he wants to do is talk?" she asked in a sulky way. "And he won't... hurt me?"

"He isn't looking to hurt you, Patty. He just wants answers. He's marrying Raina and wants to help her."

She was silent for a few seconds and then sighed. "I guess I can talk to him. But, seriously, I don't have anything more to tell him than what I told the cops."

"Then just tell him the same thing. The point is, he knows the streets and knows what the other clubs are capable of. Something you may have told the cops might make more sense to him."

"Fine. As long as he doesn't threaten me."

"He's not going to threaten you," I replied. "Tank just wants answers."

She sucked in her breath. "Oh, crap... I think he's actually calling back already. You owe me big time."

I wanted to tell her that she was the one who owed my family something, but knew it would just start another argument. "Thanks, Patty."

Mumbling something, she hung up.

I set my phone down and looked over at the clock. It was almost three in the afternoon and the longer I waited, the more I felt it was a mistake just being there. Craving a cigarette, I pulled out the pack I had in my jacket pocket and debated on lighting it. Before I could, however, the door opened and two people walked into the room. The first one being the woman from the deli.

"Hi," she said, pushing a piece of red hair behind her ear. "I have to say, I never thought I'd see you again. At least not this soon."

Eleven

TERIN

"I WAS IN the neighborhood and figured you might need my statement," he replied, his lip twitching. "And… you're welcome."

Cocky bastard.

I smirked. "Well, I do appreciate it. Thank you."

"What about Chips? Did you catch him?" asked Cole.

"No. Unfortunately, he got away," I replied, checking out the many tattoos he had on his muscular arms. He'd removed his jacket and was wearing a cut that identified him as a Gold Viper Prospect. "As did Gomer. Obviously."

"At least you know who they are." He looked at Walters. "I see you brought back-up this time."

Tearing my eyes away from his biceps, I introduced Walters.

"I think we've met," said Cole, pulling out a small lighter from the front pocket of his jeans. "You don't mind if I smoke, do you?"

"Unfortunately, there's no smoking in this building," said Walters. "And we did meet before. The night your nephew and Old Lady were shot."

"Patty is not my Old Lady," said Cole, shoving it back into his pocket, along with a pack of cigarettes.

"You two broke up?" asked Walters.

"Our relationship ended the night she brought Billy to a kegger and almost got him killed," said Cole, frowning. "I guess I should blame myself for not kicking her out of my bed after our first date."

"Do you think the guilt should only rest on her shoulders?" asked Walters.

"If she hadn't brought him there, he'd have never been shot," he said. "It's pretty obvious."

"You're not going to blame anything on yourself or your lifestyle?" asked Walters.

"What do you know of my 'lifestyle', Detective?" asked Cole.

I cleared my throat and jumped back into the conversation. "You belong to a pretty notorious club."

Cole looked at me. Unlike when he addressed Walters, there was amusement in his eyes. "Notorious for what?"

"Hell-raising," I replied, noticing the warning look that Walters was giving me.

"Hell-raising. Can you be more specific?" asked Cole innocently.

"Come off it, Johnson. You know exactly what she's talking about. But, that's not why we're here," said Walters.

"That's right. We're here to talk about the Devil's Rangers. Speaking of them, did you ever find out who the shooters were?" Cole asked.

"No," said Walters, watching him carefully. "Have you?"

"Nope," said Cole, a look of irritation flashed across his face. "Believe me, we've tried."

"Speaking of club activity, you switched sides," said Walters. "Why is that?"

"The Gold Vipers are a better fit for me," said Cole, matter-of-factly.

"And your sister is marrying the president," I said. "That would have caused a lot of tension at family gatherings."

"Definitely," said Cole, smiling slightly.

"So you did it for Raina?" asked Walters.

"I did it for myself," he replied.

"Because..?" prodded Walters, waiting for a better response.

"Just like I stated, they're a better fit. We've already established that I didn't come down here to get grilled about my club. I dropped by to help Detective O'Brien here. Do you want my statement or not?" he asked.

"Yes. We do," said Walters. "I'm going to get some coffee first. Would you like any, Mr. Johnson?"

"Yes, I could use a cup," replied Cole. "Thank you."

"How do you like it?" he asked.

"Black is fine," replied Cole.

"You want one, too?" Walters asked me.

"No. Thanks," I replied.

Walters left us alone, which I'd known that he was going to do. He thought that Cole would feel more open to talking if it was just the two of us. Pen was on the other side of the wall, listening in.

"So, why did you take off?" I asked him.

"I don't know. I guess I was hungry at the time and didn't want to spend the rest of the day down here," he said.

"But here you are anyway."

"Yep. Here I am," he replied, staring back at me.

"Well, like I said before… I do appreciate it."

"I know."

I grinned.

He smiled back. "So, how did you find yourself in that situation, anyway?"

"I was there to pick up lunch."

"And they just grabbed you?"

I knew that I could discuss what had happened before he showed up. "Something like that."

"There's more to it," he replied, studying me.

I just smiled.

"The place had been evacuated pretty quickly, it looked like to me. No customers. No staff."

I nodded. I wanted to ask him why he was there, but wasn't allowed to. His statement had to be given directly to Walters, since I was involved.

"Do you know why Pete took off with Ronnie?" he asked.

"No. I was going to ask you the same thing," I replied.

He shrugged. "My guess is that he was collecting on some kind of debt. Maybe gambling."

"So, Ronnie's a bookie?"

"Ronnie is a lot of things," he replied.

The door opened up and Walters walked in carrying two cups of coffee. He set one down in front of Cole.

"Thanks," said Cole.

"No problem," said Walters, sitting back down. He opened up a file and pulled out the paperwork for Cole's testimonial statement. "Before I forget, there's something else we need to ask you."

"What's that?" said Cole.

"Why did your sister kill Slammer?" asked Walters, as Cole raised the cup to his lips.

Twelve

COLE

I CHOKED ON the coffee. "Sorry, what was that?" I asked hoarsely.

"We received a tip today from someone claiming that she killed him," said Walters. "A phone call."

"That's bullshit," I said, knowing right away that Ronnie was behind it. "She's marrying Tank, for one. For two, my sister isn't a murderer."

"Did the Devil's Rangers put you two up to it? As an initiation into the club?" continued Walters.

"Definitely not," I said, pissed off. "Look, you and I both know this is a load of shit. Because of what happened earlier today, they're trying to pin that on me and my sister."

"Do you own a green van?" asked Walters.

The van we'd used had been 'borrowed' and since returned to the auto-body shop I worked part-time for. It had been a customer's and was back in his possession, now painted black and looking pristine. We'd actually done a complete overhaul on the vehicle. As far as I was concerned, there was no way it could be traced back to the murder, especially since I'd borrowed plates from another vehicle, earlier that morning. Even though I hadn't really expected her to shoot Slammer, I knew her head hadn't been in the

112

right place and at the time, had been more worried about the Gold Vipers finding us than the cops.

"No," I replied. "But, you already know that don't you?"

"Yes. We do," said Walters, studying my face.

"Did you trace the call that came in?" I asked.

"Yes. They used a payphone," he replied. "From Merl's Gas Station."

Merl's was one of the oldest stations in Jensen. I pictured Ronnie calling on the payphone, which was located across from the pumps.

"Have someone check the cameras," I said. "I'm sure you'll find Ronnie or one of the other members on video, making that call."

They looked at each other and Walters nodded. "We will," he replied. "No doubt about that."

"Are we done talking about this shit?" I asked, tapping my fingers on the table in frustration. "Because... if I'd have known you were going to try and pin Slammer's murder on myself or Raina, especially when I'm trying to help you guys, I'd have stayed home."

"I understand you're angry. Obviously, we had to ask," said Walters.

"You call that 'asking'?" I said, frowning. "You were basically accusing Raina. But that's how you cops operate, isn't it? Accuse and ask questions later?"

"We're trying to find a murderer," said Walters. "We do what's necessary."

"It seems to me like you should change your tactics. Accusing someone of murder, just because of an anonymous 'tip', is pretty ludicrous. Especially under the circumstances."

"It may seem that way, but our 'tactics' have proven successful in the past. You wouldn't believe the amount of criminals who want to confess, but aren't asked the right questions," said Walters. "Or hell, even asked at all."

"I doubt that Slammer's killer wants to confess, so you'd better work a lot harder than that to find out who he actually is," I replied dryly.

"Who 'she' is," said O'Brien.

"Right," I answered. "Whomever."

Walters looked at O'Brien. "Why don't you follow up on the payphone thing? See if there are any cameras pointed toward the one at the gas station."

"Will do," she said, standing up. Terin looked at me. "Thanks again for your help. All of it."

Still irritated, all I could do was nod.

She walked out of the room.

Walters handed me a form to fill out and a pen. "I'd like to second that. I'm pretty sure you saved her from being raped."

"Knowing Chips, rape was only half of it," I said. "Where do I start?"

He turned the sheet of paper over and explained how to fill it out.

"When I'm finished, am I allowed to leave?" I asked curtly.

"Of course."

"Good, because my good deed of the day seems to be biting me in the ass," I replied, picking up the pen.

"For the record, I didn't want to accuse you of anything. It's just a method we use to get a response. One we can try and read into."

"And what did you read from mine?"

"That you love your sister."

"Yes, but she isn't a killer," I said, not exactly lying. She may have murdered Slammer, but she'd not been herself. "Neither am I."

"You will be if they patch you," said Walters.

"Believe it or not, I'm with the Gold Vipers because they're not murderers."

"Son, do you really believe that?"

I wanted to tell him that if they were cold-blooded murderers, Raina wouldn't be alive. Neither would I.

"I do. The Devil's Rangers, on the other hand, they wouldn't blink an eye if they had to kill someone. They should be the ones being questioned for murder, not me. Most belong in prison."

"Is that why you're here? To help clean up the streets?" replied Walters, smirking.

I'm here because I was ordered to be here.

"I'm here for many reasons, but honestly," I pictured the scene from the deli and what might have happened if I hadn't showed up. "I'm here to make sure Chips and Gomer gets what's coming to them."

"Jail time?"

I nodded and thought of Gomer, the skinny asshole who'd once bragged about slipping some sorority chick a Mickey, so he could fuck "the snobby bitch" without resistance. "That and some extra shower time. Those two are predators. They need to see what it feels like to be victims."

"I couldn't agree more."

Thirteen

TERIN

I CALLED MERL'S station and found out from the owner's wife that they did have cameras.

"Would you be able to see the payphone?" I asked the woman.

"A little. I have to tell you, our security system is pretty old, and so are the cameras. You're welcome to take a look at the video footage though," she said.

"Thanks. I'll stop by later today," I replied and then gave her my name again.

"Sounds good. Can I ask what you're looking for?"

"We're just trying to identify a caller. You didn't happen to see anyone using the phone about an hour and a half ago?"

"If someone did, I didn't notice. One of the cashiers called in sick today and we've been pretty busy. Ten people could have used the payphone and I probably wouldn't have noticed."

"Understandable," I replied. "Well, thanks again. I'll be down as soon as I can."

"Sounds good."

We hung up and I walked back to the interrogation room just as Cole was on his way out. Behind him, still seated at the table, was Walters, talking on his cell phone.

"You're finished already?" I asked, noticing that he was holding his motorcycle helmet and leather jacket.

"Afraid so," he said, staring down at me. He stood about five inches taller than myself, and with his height and muscular frame, Cole seemed to fill the doorway.

"Oh," I answered, trying to hide my disappointment. For some reason, he intrigued me and I wanted to ask him a few more questions about his club and why joining one was so important. Instead, I stepped to the side so he could walk out of the room. As he strolled past me, I smelled motorcycle exhaust with a trace of cologne. I turned and watched him, admiring the way his jeans fit.

As if feeling my eyes on him, Cole suddenly stopped. "Did you have something else you wanted to say to me, Detective O'Brien?" he asked, turning to look at me again with those intense blue eyes.

Hot damn, he was good looking...

It was enough to almost make me understand the appeal some women had to bad boys.

I really need to get laid, I thought.

"Uh, no. I guess not. Just... thank you again for helping me at the deli," I replied, angry with myself for the way I was reacting to someone like him. "And then showing up here to give a statement."

"Not a problem."

Not even sure why, I started walking down the hallway with him.

"Detective, you know... if you really want to thank me," he said, in a low voice, "you could meet me for a drink. I think we could both use one after a day like today."

A glass of wine sounded heavenly at that moment, but I pictured the two of us in a bar together and knew it was a bad idea. Not only would it be a conflict of interest, but the fact that I was attracted to him and we'd be drinking alcohol, might lead to trouble. "A drink?"

"Yeah. Just a beer. Or, would that be too much of a crime?" he asked with a devilish grin. "Sharing a drink with someone like me?"

"Honestly, I'd like to but I can't," I admitted, realizing that I was now walking with him out of the building.

"Against the rules?" he asked as we headed toward his motorcycle.

"Yes."

"Damn," he said, giving me another killer smile, one that sent a warm, pleasurable rush to my stomach. "Well, should we ever end up at the same bar one night, and I do buy you a drink, you won't handcuff me, will you?"

I laughed. "No."

"Not that I'd mind. Hell, I'd even be open to a frisk."

"Are you flirting with me?" I asked with a wry smile as we stopped next to his bike.

"No. I'm just trying to make your job easier and if frisking does it, then I'm certainly willing to help out."

"How old are you?" I asked. I'd read that his sister was my age, which meant he was younger than me.

"I'll be twenty-four next month. I'm surprised you didn't check that," he replied.

He was two years younger. I had to admit, though, he acted more mature than some of the guys I worked with. Most of them were in their thirties and forties. "You're just a kid."

He laughed. "A kid, huh?" He studied my face. "You don't look much older than eighteen yourself, which I know you couldn't be. How old are you, if I may ask?"

"Twenty-six."

"You're kind of young for a detective, aren't you?"

"I advanced pretty quickly," I admitted. "But, I worked my ass off for it."

"I'm sure you did," he said, setting his helmet on the bike. He slipped his jacket on. "I know I wouldn't want to piss you off. Not after the way you handled Chips earlier."

"He handled me first," I replied, my smile fading. "If it wasn't for you, I doubt I would have made it out of that situation... alive."

"Honestly, I think you would have," he said. "It just would have taken longer, but you'd have gotten away."

"What is it about these clubs that interest you so much?" I asked bluntly. "I mean... why join up?"

He took a few seconds before answering. "It's about brotherhood, friendship, and camaraderie for me. Once you're accepted into a club, your brothers have your back for life, no matter the circumstances."

"So, you're joining because you want a family?"

"I have a family but I guess in a way, that's a big part of it, too. To be honest, I didn't know much about motorcycle clubs until I met Taz, a guy I used to work with. He was a Prospect for the Devil's Rangers and invited me to a party one night. Afterward, I started hanging around some of the places they frequented and got to know some of the other guys. Eventually, Taz sponsored me and I was made a Prospect."

"He must be angry that you've switched sides," I replied.

"He would be if he were still alive," said Cole, staring past me, into the distance.

"What happened to him?" I asked, wondering if he'd been murdered. I hadn't read anything about Taz in any of my reports.

"He took off one weekend to visit his parents in Texas and was killed by a drunk driver," he replied, his eyes revealing the grief he still felt. "They both died, actually."

"I'm sorry to hear that," I said, placing a hand on his forearm. "I'm sure you two were pretty close."

He stared at my hand. "He was the only guy in the Devil's Rangers with any kind of ethics. I suppose that was one thing that made it easier for me to leave the club, knowing that he was gone."

"I bet," I said, noticing some of the glances I was getting in the parking lot by other officers. I pulled my hand away. "So, you weren't that close to the other club members?"

"I was until I found out they were lying to me," he said.

"About what?"

He looked away. "Club stuff. Anyway, I'm with a better one now and have no regrets about changing. I'm just grateful Tank didn't hold my prior club affiliation against me."

"I'm sure marrying your sister gave you a free pass, too," I replied.

"No. There are never free passes into anything. You have to prove your loyalty," said Cole.

"How do you have to prove it?" I asked, knowing that for many clubs, it meant doing something illegal.

Cole swung his leg over his bike and sat down. "I'm still trying to figure that out."

Fourteen

COLE

"**H**OPEFULLY, YOU WON'T be doing anything that will land you behind bars," she replied.

I smiled and started the bike. "You sound like my Uncle Sal."

"And he sounds like an intelligent guy. Nice motorcycle, by the way," she said loudly.

"You ride?"

"No."

"Have you ever been on a bike?"

"When I was young, my father used to take me for rides on his."

"What kind did he have?"

"He owned a Gold Wing."

I nodded and asked if she wanted to take a ride with me.

Terin looked around the parking lot and then back to me. She looked uncomfortable. "I have to get back to work."

"What about when you're off?"

"I really can't."

"I could pick you up at your place. Nobody would have to know," I said. I'd noticed the way her eyes had lit up at the mention of a ride and knew she wanted to.

126

"Seriously, Cole, I can't and you know why. Anyway," she began backing away. "Thanks again for stopping by and filling out the report."

She was right. I knew it was a long shot but I couldn't help myself. She was a sexy little number and I hadn't been laid in a couple of weeks. The thought of taking her back to my place and giving her my own ride was enough to make my jeans tight.

"Too bad," I said, revving the engine a little. "One ride with me on a Harley, and I guarantee you'd never want to get off." I gave her a wicked grin. "At least not without me."

She smiled. "You're pretty sure of yourself, aren't you?"

"Only when it comes to things that I want."

"And what is that?" she asked, looking flushed.

My eyes trailed up and down her body, making it obvious as to what I wanted.

Her blush deepened. "Goodbye, Cole," she said, backing away.

"If you need me for anything else, you have my number," I told her. "Case related or personal."

"I'll keep that in mind."

I slipped the helmet over my head. "I'll definitely be keeping you in mind."

"Am I the first cop you've ever flirted with?" she asked.

I grinned. "Does Walters count?"

Laughing, she turned and walked back toward the building.

Fifteen

TERIN

I WAS STILL grinning to myself when I heard the rumble of Cole's bike as he took off. I had to admit, he sure knew how to make a woman laugh. I had a feeling he knew how to make her do a lot of other things as well.

When I returned to the building, Walters called me into his office.

"What's up?" I asked, sitting down.

"Did you call Merl's?" he asked, leaning back in his squeaky chair.

"Yes, they do have working cameras, although I was told that they were pretty old." I'd been so involved with Cole that I'd almost forgotten about the video footage. "I'm going to head there right now and see what's on them."

"Okay. And... O'Brien?"

"Yes?"

He gave me a funny smile. "You do realize that Cole Johnson, as much as he helped us today, is off limits."

"Sir, what do you mean?" I asked, staring at him in surprise.

"Bronson saw you out in the parking lot with him."

"So? I walked him out to his bike. We were discussing his decision on joining a motorcycle club," I said, angry that Bronson wasn't just spying on me, but reporting back to Walters.

He nodded. "Just be careful."

"If anyone should be careful, it's Bronson," I muttered.

Nodding, Walters took a sip of his coffee. "I agree. I had a feeling that he was just trying to start trouble, but wanted to talk to you about it anyway. You're an intelligent woman and a damned good cop. Not somebody who'd mingle with scum like Johnson."

"Exactly," I said. "I admit, we talked for a while. I just wanted to know what the appeal is to these clubs."

"And I suppose he gave you the old 'friendship and camaraderie' spiel."

I nodded.

"It's not just that. They could find that by joining a church or bowling league. These guys love the attention and the danger involved with belonging to a club like the Devil's Rangers and Gold Vipers."

"Aren't the Gold Vipers pretty clean compared to the Devil's Rangers?" I asked.

"That's what they want you to believe but… that's bullshit. If they were upstanding and law-abiding citizens, there wouldn't be so many dead Devil's Rangers, now would there?"

He had a point. There was no arguing that in the last three years, there'd been a slew of deaths, including a guy name Mud, the Hayward president, and Jon Hughes, the head of the Mother Charter.

"If anything, the Gold Vipers are even more dangerous. Not only are they smarter, but much more cunning. That's why we brought you on, O'Brien. We need all the support we can get when it comes to catching these guys, and believe me… we will."

I nodded.

"Now, obviously we won't be sending you in undercover. Not after what happened today."

"I understand," I replied.

"Oh, by the way, they've already arrested Chips and Gomer."

I sighed in relief. "What about Ronnie?"

"Not yet, but they're working on it."

"And what of Pete?"

"Nothing yet," said Walters.

"Did anyone check to see if there was activity in Pete's checking or savings account?"

He nodded. "No activity, which isn't surprising since he doesn't have much in his accounts. Maybe two hundred dollars at the most."

My eyes widened. "But, his deli must be doing well, right?"

"One would think. However, if he was anxious about meeting with Ronnie, then it's obvious that he's having financial difficulties."

"Cole thought that Ronnie might have been collecting on a gambling debt."

"I'm thinking the same thing."

"Is Pete married?"

"He's divorced," he replied.

My phone began to vibrate. I pulled it out of my pocket and noticed that I'd received a text from my sister:

CALL ME!

"You'd better get a move on," said Walters, turning back to his laptop. "And buzz me as soon as you find the video footage."

"I will," I replied, stepping out of his office. Noticing that Bronson was the only one sitting at his desk, I refrained from ripping him a new asshole and went over to my desk to grab my purse.

"Where you off to, O'Brien?" asked Bronson, obviously ready to push more of my buttons.

I turned around and gave him a dirty look. "I'm going to Merl's Gas Station to check on the video footage of the person who called in the tip on Slammer's murderer. Why?"

He smirked. "Just curious. Looks like you made a new friend today."

"What are you talking about?"

"Cole Johnson. I saw the way you two were looking at each other outside in the parking lot. Like you were ready to tear each other's clothes off."

My face grew hot. "That's bullshit, Bronson. Whatever you think you saw, is something your twisted mind created. Probably because I rejected you."

Bronson stood up. "You'd better stop right there," he said, leaning forward on his desk.

I walked closer and looked him dead in the eye. "No, you're the one who'd better stop before you find your ass out of a job."

He laughed coldly. "You think you can threaten me?"

"I'm not threatening you. I'm telling you exactly how it is. You know, it was bad enough having you grope me, but now to have to deal with these bullshit lies of yours to get me into trouble. You'd better back off, Bronson, or I'll-"

"You'll what?" he asked with a sneer.

Suddenly remembering my voice recorder, I reached into my pocket and pressed record. "Make it so that one day you'll wish you still had your wife, your balls, *and* your job back."

"Listen, you little bitch," he said in a low, threatening voice. "I've been working here a lot longer than you have and there were no witnesses, so my job is secure. As far as touching you, I bet that's the only action you've gotten for a long, long time because you're such a frigid little bitch."

Trying to remain calm, I began counting backwards from ten. I needed him to keep going. And being the condescending, disgusting asshole that he was, he did.

"You know, you should get down on your knees and thank me for it," he sneered.

Trying not to gloat too much, I pulled the audio recorder and held it up. "You know, I won't get down on my knees, but I do want to thank you," I said, ending the recording. "For being so predictable."

"What the fuck is that?" he growled, trying to grab it from me.

"A mini voice recorder," I said, backing away with a triumphant grin. "And proof that you're a disgusting pig."

"You can't use that against me, you know. It would be inadmissible in court."

"I'm not looking to use it in court," I replied. "But I'm sure your wife would be interested in listening to it. So would Walters."

His face turned red with rage.

"Like I said before, don't fuck with me and I won't fuck with you. Understand, Bronson?"

He didn't say anything.

"Bronson?" I repeated, looking him dead in the eye. "I'm not dishing out idle threats. Do you understand?"

Still staring at me with hatred, he could only nod.

"Good." I pulled the strap of my purse over my shoulder, turned around, and walked away. It was a small victory but I couldn't help but feel like a weight had been lifted from my shoulders.

Sixteen

COLE

AFTER LEAVING THE police station, I drove back to the clubhouse. Tank was still there, talking with Raptor and Tail at the bar.

"Where've you been all day, slacker?" joked Tail, holding a beer.

I smirked. "Cleaning up all the condoms you left in the parking lot last night. You know, correct me if I'm wrong, but I don't think you can catch STDs from beating off."

"You can if you're Tail," said Raptor, cracking up. "Lord only knows where those fingers have been."

Tail flipped us both off. "At least I'm getting laid. You're married so I know you're not seeing any action," he said to Raptor and then turned to me with a grin. "And you? You have no excuses... unless your dick is as lame as your jokes."

"I think the problem is that my dick has shriveled up inside of me, since I've been so busy being all of your bitches."

They laughed.

Raptor reached into the cooler and popped open a beer. "We've all been there, brother," he said, handing it to me. "Just hang tight and keep doing what you're doing. Soon enough you'll be recruiting your own Prospects and putting them to work."

"Speaking of work, you free tonight? I need you bouncing at Griffin's," said Tank.

"Yeah, I'm free," I replied.

"If you're lucky, one of the dancers will help retract your unit and make you a man again," said Tank.

"I suggest Candy," said Tail. "The new chick. If anyone can give you wood, it's her."

"You fucked Candace already?" asked Tank.

"Let's just say that I played me some Candy-land last weekend. Spent me some time in Gum Drop Hills. A little while later, she made it to Lollipop Forest, after which..." he grinned wickedly, "I blew my load over at Ice Cream River."

We all groaned.

"Thanks, man. I'll never be able to play that game again without thinking like a perv," said Raptor, who had a two-year-old son.

"You should try playing it with just Adriana," said Tank, grinning. "I bet she'd finally let you into her castle again."

"Might not be a bad idea," he answered.

"What's up? You two having problems?" asked Tail.

"No. She's just been so tired lately," he answered.

"Maybe she's pregnant?" suggested Tank.

Raptor scratched his chin and nodded. "Huh, I never thought of that."

"You guys know that we didn't really use the board game," explained Tail. "Right?"

I snorted. "No, shit, really?"

"I knew that the moment you got the locations wrong," said Raptor.

"Funny because I seemed to hit the right locations with her," said Tail, taking another swig of his beer.

"Okay. Enough about your sex life," said Tank. "Some of us haven't eaten for a while."

"What's wrong, Prez? You missing your bachelor lifestyle already?" asked Tail.

"Fuck no," said Tank. "I got a horny little woman who can't keep her hands off of me. Even if I was offered new pussy on a platter, I'd be too exhausted to take a bite." Tank looked at me. "Not that I'd cheat on Raina, brother."

"Hey, no worries man. What happens between the two of you is your business," I replied.

"I know, but I have a sister myself and I'd want to beat the fuck out of anyone who hurt her," he replied.

"I didn't say I wouldn't want to pound your head in," I told him with a smile. "I'd just step back and let you two work it out."

"Raina would kick my ass," said Tank, smiling. "And I'd deserve it. Anyway, we should talk about your meeting downtown. Let's go back to my office."

"What happened downtown?" asked Tail.

"I'll fill you and everyone else in later," Tank answered.

"Okay," said Tail, his eyes glossy.

"How many beers have you had?" I asked.

"Just a couple, *mom*," he replied dryly.

"Don't go anywhere," said Tank, also noticing that Tail was buzzed. "I'll have someone give you a ride home."

Tail smiled and took another drink of beer. "My ride should be on her way any minute."

"Another date?" asked Hoss, who was just walking out of the bathroom.

"I don't know if I'd call it a date," he replied. "We're going back to her place and she's going to give me a rub-down."

"A rub-down?" repeated Hoss.

"She's going to school to become a masseuse. I'm letting her practice on me. It's the least I can do," he said, smiling.

"Where do you find these chicks?" asked Raptor.

"Tail is like the Pied Piper of Pussy," said Hoss, shaking his head. "The lucky son-of-a-bitch."

"Wait a second. What happened to your Facebook friend from earlier?" asked Tail.

"Lana? That fucking bitch really was trying to steal money from me. Lucky for her she's in another country or I'd drive to where she was and teach her a fucking lesson," he said, looking pissed.

"At least she didn't get anything from you," said Tank.

"She did get something from me," said Hoss. "My time, which is valuable." He cracked his knuckles. "Anyway, I just deleted my account so I don't get any other crackpots trying to 'friend' me."

"Good idea," said Tank, patting him on the shoulder. "You can't trust anyone on the internet these days."

"Or on the streets," said Hoss. "The world is going to pot."

"You know, they do have those dating sites," said Tail. "You want to meet a woman, and are looking for more than sex, you should check those out."

"I want sex, but I'd also like to meet someone with the same kind of interests," he replied.

"Then you should look into it. I heard that you can pretty much list the kind of qualities you like in a chick and they'll match you with someone."

Hoss's face brightened. "Really?"

"Oh hell," groaned Tank, rolling his eyes. Here we go again." He nodded toward me. "Let's get out of here before I have to listen to Hoss's 'requirements'."

"I'm not fussy," said Hoss. "I just need a woman who likes motorcycles and doesn't yet have breasts staring down at her navel."

Chuckling, I stood up. "That's all, huh?"

"Maybe someone who can cook and not just frozen meals," he replied, scratching his whiskers. "Casseroles, pot roasts, and... pie. Haven't had me a homemade apple pie for ages."

"Had me some pie last night," said Tail, chuckling.

Hoss gave him the finger.

Seventeen

TERIN

AS I MADE my way out to the parking lot, I called my sister. "What's up?"

"I just found out what happened earlier from watching the news. Why didn't you call me?!"

"Sorry. I've been so busy," I replied, frowning. It was on the news already? "Mom doesn't know about it, does she?"

"Did you hear from her?"

"No."

"Then you know that she hasn't. I think it's her hair appointment day."

I sighed. "Okay. I should probably call her and let her know before she turns on the television later."

"Do you think?" she reply dryly.

I ignored the sarcasm. "Anyway, I have to go. Can I call you later?"

"Yes. Are you okay?"

"I'm fine."

"Did they catch the guys yet?"

"Two of them."

"How many were there?"

"Three in all."

"We get lunch there all the time. I can't believe it. I suppose you can't talk too much about it."

"You got it."

"I understand. You're still going to make it on Saturday, right?"

"Yes. Of course."

"By the way, Mom wants to go."

"To the bachelorette party?" I asked, shocked.

"I know, right? She asked if there were going to be strippers." She laughed. "I think that's why she wants to be there. I don't think she's seen a naked man in years."

I pictured our prim and proper mother passing out dollars to a bunch of hard-bodied men and it made me giggle. "*Are* there going to be strippers?"

"Beats me. All I know is that one of my friends, Sheila, reserved a party bus."

"Actually, I hope she does join us. I think she'd have fun, strippers or not."

"I think she's really going to come. She also asked if Frannie could join us."

"Frannie?" My eyes widened. "Are we talking about the same woman who was married to Slammer?"

"Yes. Apparently, they used to work together at the nursing home. I had no idea. Anyway, Mom thinks that it would do her some good, especially now that her husband is gone. Plus, I think she's going to feel more comfortable with someone closer to her age."

I wasn't sure if interacting with anyone affiliated with the Gold Vipers was a good idea. At least for me, because of my position. But, I also wanted my mother to enjoy herself and I was a little intrigued with meeting the woman. As if reading my mind, my sister reminded me that Frannie wasn't an actual member of the club.

"I guess it would be okay," I replied.

"Are you sure? If you're worried about it, we don't have to invite her."

"No. It's fine." I decided that if Walters found out about it and had a problem, I'd remind him that I was off duty and couldn't control who my sister invited to her bachelorette party.

"Okay. I'll let her know. Anyway, I know you're busy and so am I. Call me later, okay?"

"I will."

After we hung up, I called my mother's cell phone and left a message. I gave her a quick summary of what happened and told her that I was fine and would call her later. Then, I drove to Merl's Gas Station, where Helga, the owner's wife, showed me how to check the video surveillance cameras. It didn't take long before I found what I was looking for. Unfortunately, the footage was so poor that it was hard to make out exactly who the man was on the payphone. Not surprised but still frustrated, I took out my cell phone and called Walters.

"What did you find?" he asked.

I stared at the image on the video and sighed. "A man on a motorcycle, wearing a dark leather jacket, is really all that I'm sure of. It doesn't look as if there are any club patches on the back of it, though. Other than that, there isn't anything recognizable. It certainly doesn't look like Ronnie, Chips, or Gomer."

"How can you be sure it's not one of them if the image is so shitty?"

"His frame, I guess, and the way he was standing."

"What kind of a bike did he pull up on?"

I'd been doing some research on motorcycles and recognized the style. "Looks like a Harley. I'd say it's a Dyna."

"Newer?"

"Um… maybe a couple of years old, although, again, it's hard to tell."

"Fairing?"

"Yes."

"Gauntlet?"

"What?" I asked.

"It's the style of fairing. Another common one they seem to like is the Batwing. That's what Gomer had on his bike when we picked him up."

"I really have no clue. Sorry."

"Okay, back to the driver... what about his hair or facial features?"

"He's too far away. The only thing I can tell you is that he's wearing a helmet and that," I looked closer at the image I'd paused. "He might be a little stocky."

"Fat?"

"I'm thinking a thicker belly. His legs are thin but his jacket seems to be fitting pretty tightly."

"Hmm... how old do you think he is?"

I stared at the biker's frame. "I don't know. I'd say he's over thirty. Maybe even in his forties or fifties."

"How can you tell?"

"The way his jeans are fitting and his legs look very skinny. Also, when he walked around the bike, he seemed to be limping a little."

"Limping?"

"Yeah. Just slightly," I said, rewinding the tape again to see him walk. "If I were to guess, he's got a bad knee or one leg is shorter than the other."

Walters grunted. "Good eye, O'Brien. Anything else?"

"Not really. Like I said, the footage is pretty poor."

"Okay then. Bring it in and we'll have someone analyze it."

"Is that really necessary?" I asked. "I mean, patches or not, you and I both know that it was a Devil's Ranger who called in the bogus tip. Obviously, Cole and Raina had nothing to do with the shooting."

"Probably not, but we still need to check it out."

"*Probably* not?"

"Never assume anything, O'Brien. That's when you put your blinders on and miss what might be staring at you in the face."

As far as I was concerned, we were wasting time with the video footage and needed to open our eyes to other possibilities. The Devil's Rangers surely had a lot of enemies, not just the Gold Vipers. But, he was the boss.

"Okay, I'll bring it in," I replied.

"Good. By the way, we've got Chips and Gomer right now, sitting in separate interrogation rooms."

"Are they saying anything?"

"No. This obviously isn't their first trip down here. Anyway, both of them are waiting on their lawyers."

I sighed. I hadn't really expected them to admit to anything, but I wasn't looking forward to a long, drawn-out attempted assault case. "Any word on Pete or Ronnie?"

"Nope. He's not at the clubhouse either. We still have an APB out. Hopefully we'll find them soon."

"What about their club president?"

"Schmitty? Apparently that douchebag is on a cross-country road trip and unreachable. The rest of the club members are keeping a tight lip and claim they know nothing about Pete or the deli incident."

No surprise there, I thought.

"Did you find any cameras in the deli?" I asked.

"Yes, but they weren't turned on. Looks like he hasn't used them in quite a while."

"What about the back alley, behind the deli?"

"Nothing back there, but we have you as a witness. If Pete is dead and Ronnie was the last one seen with him, *and* threatening him with a gun, we should have enough to charge him."

Maybe, but even I knew that when it came to putting a criminal behind bars and keeping him there, nothing ever went smoothly.

Eighteen

COLE

"SO, HOW DID it go?" asked Tank, leading me back into his office.

"It went okay, although... someone from the Devil's Rangers called in a tip about Raina shooting your old man."

"Assholes," he muttered, sitting down. He ran a hand over his face. "What did the cops say about that?"

"They think it's bullshit," I said, sitting down across from him. "Especially since you two are getting married."

Tank, always concerned that someone might be bugging his office, grabbed a piece of paper and wrote down something. Then handed it to me. In the note he asked if the Devil's Rangers knew Raina had actually done it.

I nodded.

He let out a ragged sigh and then wrote down something else.

Is there any evidence that could link her to the crime?

I shook my head.

"You sure?" he asked out loud.

"Everything has been taken care of."

"Let's hope so."

Even I had to admit that it was weird hearing those words coming from the victim's son. We sat there

153

silently for a few minutes and then he asked me more about my meeting with the cops. I told him everything.

"You know they're going to keep trying to pin my old man's death on you two," he said. "Especially after what happened today."

"Oh yeah. I know."

He grunted. "You think they were mad before, I'm sure Ronnie and Schmitty are foaming at the mouth right about now. Especially if Ronnie's killed Pete. Obviously, they weren't expecting any living witnesses."

"Hell no. They would have killed Terin for sure if I hadn't stepped inside of that deli."

Tank's phone began to ring. He looked at the caller ID. "It's Raina," he said and then answered it. They exchanged a few words and then he told her he'd be home late.

"Club business. It shouldn't take too long," he said, looking at me.

She said something else.

"Yeah, he's here right now. You want to talk to him? Okay." He handed the phone to me.

"Hey, Raina. What's up?"

"I went and visited Uncle Sal. He's starting to look better," she answered.

"Good to hear."

"He sends his love."

"Okay. I'll have to try and stop by tomorrow. I'm glad that he's doing better at least."

She sighed. "Yes. I spoke to his doctor and he's on a waiting list for a new liver."

"How long is the wait?" I asked.

"He didn't give me an actual timeframe, but mentioned the list of people is pretty long... in the thousands."

"How do we get him to the top of the list?" I asked, horrified.

"There's nothing we can do," she said sadly. "All I know is that the people on the top are the ones that are the most critical. Then, it depends on blood type, age, and all of that."

I sighed.

"Face it, there's nothing that we can do but wait and make sure that he doesn't drink anymore."

I agreed.

"So, not to change the subject but is everything okay with the club?"

"Everything is fine," I replied.

"Tank wouldn't tell me anything about earlier."

"Not much to tell," I replied.

"I bet. I know very well that he's sitting right there," she scolded. "And probably making sure that you don't spill any beans."

I looked at Tank, who was actually doodling some picture of a naked chick on scratch paper. "I'll have you know he's not even paying attention. In fact, he's working on his artistic abilities."

Tank smiled.

"He is, huh? He'd better not be trying out that new body paint on one of the strippers," she said firmly.

"Body paint?" I repeated, my eyes widening. "What?"

Tank began to laugh. "Oh shit. She thinks I was serious."

I had no idea what either of them were talking about and I wasn't about to talk to my sister about body paint. I handed him the phone. "I think you'd better talk to her. She sounds like she's getting pissed."

Tank took the phone. "Raina... hey, listen to me, darlin', I was just teasing you the other day. I ordered the body paint for us. You and me. Not the strippers."

She said something on the other end and it didn't sound good.

"I had it shipped to the bar so I could claim it on my taxes. Yes... It's a tax write-off if I do it that way. Anyway, babe, even if it was for them, I wouldn't be the one applying it. I'd probably let you do it. Now *that* would be hot."

I snorted.

"I gotta go," said Tank. "I'll pick up Billy from Frannie's and we'll bring you dinner tonight. How late are you working at the bar?"

Raina said something and Tank nodded.

"Okay. See you then. Love you," Tank said, smiling into the phone. He hung up and looked at me. "I'm glad you didn't fill her in on today's events. She knows something went down, and knowing your sister, she'll try prying it out of me using food or sex."

"I didn't need to know that."

He laughed.

"Speaking of prying things out of people, did you get any information from Patty?"

"Not yet. I'm going to see if I can catch her at Rumors, Saturday night."

"No sooner, huh?"

"I've got other things going on until then."

"You bringing Raina?"

"Hell no. Even I know that's a bad idea," said Tank. "She'd probably beat the shit out of her and get us kicked out of the place."

"Hell yeah, she would."

"Of course, watching two chicks brawl is hot," said Tank.

"Normally, yeah, but we're talking about my sister," I replied.

He chuckled. "I see where you're coming from. Anyway, don't forget about working at Griffin's tonight."

"What time do you need me?"

"Nine."

"Okay."

"I appreciate it," he said. "By the way, I know you've got Saturday night off, so if you want to join us at Rumors, be my guest."

"Thanks. I'll have to think about that one," I replied. "I'm trying to avoid Patty."

"She's that bad, huh?"

"Worse," I replied. "And she still wants me back."

"You still have feelings for her?"

"Not any good ones."

He chuckled.

Nineteen

TERIN

I **RETURNED TO** the precinct with the video footage and ran into Fred, who was leaving for the day.

"They arrested and booked those two bikers who attacked you in the deli," he said, pulling his car keys out of his jacket pocket.

"I heard. Did their attorney show up yet?"

He nodded. "They're speaking with him right now. Both of their hearings are scheduled for Thursday morning."

"Any news on the deli owner?"

"Nothing on Pete yet and Ronnie is still on the loose."

"I figured as much. Well, have a good night," I said.

"You, too. Go home and get some rest," he ordered with a smile.

"I'll try," I told him.

After what had happened that day, I knew sleep wouldn't come easy. At least not without a couple glasses of wine.

I took the elevator to the third floor and walked directly into Walters's office, ignoring Bronson, who was seated across from him and glowering.

"You're back. Good," said Walters. "We were just talking about you."

160

"Really? About what?" I asked, my eye twitching. From the look on Bronson's face, I wondered if he'd told him about our conversation earlier. From what I could tell, Walters was smart enough to know what kind of shithead he really was.

"Today's incident made television already," he replied. "Channel Twelve News."

I relaxed. "Yeah, I already heard. What did they say about it?"

"Not much, although they located the deli cashier who waited on you. She gave a short interview, mentioning you and the Devil's Rangers. She basically told them what she told us."

"And what was that, exactly?" I asked, not having spoken to her since the incident.

"That two bikers showed up, looking for Pete. She felt that his life was in danger and now he's missing. She also explained that you took over the situation, ordered her to call the police, and cleared out the place. That's basically it in a nutshell."

I nodded.

Walters pointed toward the bag I was holding. "Is that the surveillance video?"

"Oh, yes." I handed it to him.

"Great. I'll have it analyzed and see if we can figure out who the caller was. In the meantime, why don't you head out and get some rest?" he said. "You've had a rough day."

161

It was just past six p.m. and admittedly, I was beat. "Okay."

He studied my face. "Actually, why don't you take tomorrow off as well?"

"No. I'll be fine. Besides, I need to be at the hearing tomorrow morning."

"Isn't your sister's bachelorette party this weekend?" he asked, smiling. "Now that sounds like a crime scene waiting to happen."

I grinned. "Oh, so you've met my sister and her friends?"

Walters chuckled. "Sounds like your weekend is going to be crazy. Well, you're young and deserve to let loose once in a while."

He was probably right, although I'd always been more of a homebody. It was probably because of my career, but more than anything, I preferred my nights quiet and stress free. Admittedly, it wasn't much fun spending those nights alone. "Maybe. Anyway, could you let me know if and when they find Ronnie?"

"We'll keep you posted. I'm about ready to head out of myself soon," said Walters, looking at his watch.

"Okay. I guess I'll see you tomorrow then," I replied.

"Have a good night," he answered.

Still ignoring Bronson, I wished Walters the same and then left the office.

On my way home, I stopped at the grocery store and picked up a few items. When I arrived at my apartment, my cell phone began to buzz. It was my mother.

"Hi, Mom."

"Hi, sweetheart. Are you still working?"

"No. I'm home now."

She let out a ragged sigh. "I got your message. I'm so relieved that you're okay. You *are* okay, right?"

"I'm fine," I answered as I unpacked my groceries.

"They didn't really say much on the news. What happened?"

I gave her a brief rundown, leaving out the part where they were talking about raping me. She didn't need to know that.

"Thank goodness for that young man who walked into the deli. Who was he?"

"A guy named Cole." I explained that he was a member of the Gold Vipers. "Don't say anything to anyone, Mom. I probably shouldn't even be talking to you about it."

"You know me. I know how to keep my mouth shut," she replied.

Which was why I told her almost everything. Unlike my sister, our mother was good at keeping secrets. She worked part-time as a grief counselor. Prior to that, a child psychiatrist. She knew the importance of confidentiality.

"Yes, I do. Anyway, like I said, I'm fine and they now have two of the men in custody."

"What about the owner of the deli? Have they found him yet?"

"No," I replied.

"So, they were members of the Devil's Rangers, huh? Did I tell you that I'm friends with Frannie Fleming? She was married to a member of the Gold Vipers."

"Yeah. I know. Slammer. He was the president," I replied. "I spoke to Torie earlier about her. I heard that you two are planning on being at the bachelorette party."

"I'm not sure yet. I asked her and she said she'd need to think about it. To tell you the truth, the only reason why I thought of going in the first place was to try and cheer her up."

"I heard that you two used to work together at the nursing home," I said.

"Yes. She just quit recently. To take care of her new grandson, Billy."

Raina's boy.

"What is she like?" I asked.

"Frannie is a sweetheart. Always polite and friendly to everyone. Honestly, when I learned that she was married to one of the Gold Vipers, I was quite shocked."

"Why? Because she isn't your average biker chick?" I asked, amused.

"Yes, and that's an understatement."

"Do you know how they met?"

She laughed. "At church."

My eyes widened. "Church?"

"Yes. They met during a Bingo game and started talking. I don't think she realized who he was at the time. Anyway, he was very nice to her and had her laughing so hard, that she almost peed her pants, I guess," said my mother, a smile in her voice.

"Do you think that changed after they tied the knot? Her laughing?" I asked wryly.

"I don't think so. She made a comment once that he never brought any of his troubles home with him. Even when she knew that things were tough, he wanted to protect her and Jessica."

"Who's Jessica?" I asked.

"Her daughter."

I hadn't heard anything about Slammer having a step-daughter. Interesting.

"She's been staying with Frannie, but I heard she's moving to Minnesota soon, to begin her internship as a nurse."

"Oh. I wonder if we should invite her to the bachelorette party?"

"I guess she's in Vegas right now. Oh, I'm getting another call. It's from Torie."

"Okay."

"Call me tomorrow and let me know what's going on with the case and if they find the deli owner." She sighed. "I hope he's not dead."

"I hope not either. Goodbye, Mom."

"Goodbye. I love you."

"Love you, too."

After I hung up the phone, I made myself a large salad and then decided to go to the gym. It had been a couple of weeks since I'd last visited, and after struggling to chase down Chips, I knew I needed to get back on the treadmill.

After I finished my dinner, I put on a pair of white nylon shorts and a blue tank. Then I filled a water bottle, slipped on my tennis shoes, and headed out.

I arrived at Total Gym just after seven-thirty. It was packed and there was a wait for the treadmills. In the meantime, I decided to do some strength training, so I headed over to the weight area and started looking through the dumbbells.

"We've got to stop meeting like this," said a familiar voice behind me.

I turned around and couldn't help but gape at Cole, who stood there wearing black shorts and a white tank top that showed off his hot bod. He was holding two enormous dumbbells and his face and muscles glistened with sweat.

I laughed nervously. "Oh, wow. I didn't know you worked out here."

"I usually do it in the morning, but didn't have time to today," he said, setting the weights down. He removed his shirt and wiped the sweat from his face. "How about you?"

My mouth went dry as I stared lustfully at his sexy pecs and abs.

How long had it been since I'd had sex?

Too long. Much too long...

"Detective?" he said.

My eyes met his and I could tell that he'd caught me checking him out.

My face burned with embarrassment.

Twenty

COLE

HELL **YEAH**, I knew she was checking me out. I couldn't help but do the same.

Terin lowered her eyes and told me that she usually worked out in the evenings.

"I've been slacking lately, though," she said, placing a hand on her stomach. "I need to get back into shape."

From where I was standing, her shape looked mighty fine to me. She was curvy, yes, but in all the right places. It was especially noticeable with the tank she had on and shorts, which showed off a nice set of legs.

"I'm sure if I told you that you don't look like you've been slacking, it would sound like a come-on. So... I'll just keep my opinions to myself," I answered.

"Considering our conversation earlier, yes. But... thanks for the compliment," she said, looking pleased. She nodded toward me. "You look like you're able to fit in time here relatively often."

"I get here when I can," I said, glancing over at the clock. My shift at Griffin's started at nine and it was almost eight.

Fuck. Now I didn't want to leave.

"So, do you normally use a personal trainer?" I asked her.

"No. I typically just get on the treadmill, but since they're all full at the moment, decided to try my luck over here." She looked down at the five pound weights she was still holding and smiled. "I don't really know what I'm doing, to be honest."

"If you'd like, I can show you some basic moves for toning up your arms and torso. I used to work as a personal trainer, part time."

"Okay. Thank you."

"No problem," I said and then proceeded to show her how to do basic dumbbell curls.

As she was doing them, she glanced down at her chest. "My sister stopped using weights, complaining that she toned up but lost in places she didn't want to lose. I guess that's why I've always shied away from lifting. It's not like I have a lot to begin with," she mused.

My eyes moved to her breasts. I wasn't sure what she was talking about. From what I could tell, Terin's were more than a handful, which was all that was needed.

"Lifting weights will definitely raise your metabolism and you'll burn fat, even when you're not moving," I said. "Obviously, it will probably include some breast tissue. That being said, even if you shrink a little I'm sure yours will still be perfect."

She blushed. "Perfect? Right."

170

"Don't let your back slouch," I said, moving closer to her.

Terin brought her shoulders back, straightening her posture.

"There you go. Just do five more reps," I said, staring at her perky tits. They were rising and falling with every rep. I imagined cupping both of them in my hands, and it gave me an instant boner.

"Five more?" she repeated.

"Yes. You're doing great," I replied, moving behind her so she couldn't see my hard-on.

"Okay," she said, staring at her reflection in the mirror.

Our eyes met for a brief second in the mirror before she looked away. I looked at her chest again and noticed that her nipples were rock hard.

Fuck.

I wanted her so badly that even my balls ached. Unable to help myself, I leaned closer to her. "By the way, Detective," I whispered in a husky voice, "if it's one thing I do know, it's breasts. And I meant it when I said... yours are perfect."

Twenty – one

TERIN

HIS BREATH WAS hot on my neck as he said the words and it sent shivers all the way down to my pelvis.

"Well, thank you," I said, laughing nervously. I quickly moved away and set the weights down. "Actually I think I'm good with strength training for today."

"You didn't finish," he said, looking disappointed.

"My arms are sore already," I lied, running a hand over my bicep. "Don't want to tear anything, right?"

"True and you should stretch out your arm muscles, or they'll be sore tomorrow."

"Okay. What do you recommend?"

He showed me some arm stretches that I'd seen before but somehow looked better on him. Torn between jumping his bones and running like hell, I followed his instructions and did some stretching.

"You sure you don't want to try something else? We could work out your triceps next. Or your deltoids?" he said, bending down to pick up his tank top from the floor.

I stared at his nice, firm butt and imagined what it would be like to work the muscle hidden in the front of his shorts. The thought made my lady parts flutter. "No, I'm good."

He turned around and sighed. "I should probably get going anyway. I need to take a shower before heading to work."

I imagined his muscular body in the shower, naked and hard. I decided to buy batteries on the way home from the gym. For my vibrator.

"You okay?" he asked, giving me a funny look.

"Just a little out of breath from doing reps," I lied. I laughed nervously. "I really am out of shape."

"If you ever do need a personal trainer, or just want someone to work out with, give me a call," he said, giving me another of his sexy smiles. "We can hook up anytime."

My eyebrow arched. "Hook up?"

His grin widened. "I still meant working out but if you need help in that area too, I'd be more than happy to oblige."

As manly and sexy as he was, I knew that sleeping with Cole Johnson would be a horrible mistake. I could even lose my job.

"I'm going to forget that comment, so it's not awkward between us," I replied, trying to appear unaffected. "Especially if we run into each other again."

"I'm sure we will, Detective," he said, walking back over to where I stood. "And as far as having an awkward moment," he placed his hand against the wall and leaned into me, "I don't think you can get any more awkward than a man with a raging hard-on for a woman who wants it, but is too chicken to do anything about it."

Thank goodness there wasn't anyone near us. I swallowed. "And... how do you know what I want?" I asked, my pulse racing.

"It's in your eyes," he said, staring into them. Then he looked at my lips. "In the way you're breathing."

I sucked in my breath and held it.

He gave me a wicked grin and traced his finger along my arm, giving me goosebumps. "And in the way your nipples are begging for attention," he whispered, the side of his hand brushing against my breast.

He was right.

They wanted his mouth. His tongue.

Getting no resistance from me, Cole's hand dropped to my shorts and I felt his finger lightly stroke my thigh. "Something tells me that there's more evidence down yonder."

My womanhood ached with need and I wanted nothing more than to hump his leg like a bitch in heat.

"What do you say, Detective? Should I follow my hunch?"

I looked around, noticing that the only other person in the weight room was a muscular young man doing leg presses. He wasn't paying us any mind, and I was so horny that my own was racing with irrational thoughts, like dragging Cole into one of the supply

175

rooms and having my way with him. Thankfully, before I could give in to my reckless needs, my cell phone rang.

"Excuse me," I said breathlessly, moving away from him.

Cole sighed.

Twenty-two

two

COLE

AS SHE WALKED away, I vowed that one way or another, I was going to have her. Unfortunately, it wasn't going to be anytime soon.

Terin answered the phone and a puzzled look spread across her face. "Who is this?" she asked, frowning.

The caller said something else and hung up.

"What's going on?" I asked.

"Nothing," she said, putting her phone away.

From the expression on her face, I could tell that she'd been rattled by the caller.

"You okay?"

"Yeah. I'm fine."

"Who called you?"

"Some prank caller."

"Oh. Okay." I glanced at the clock and noticed how late it was. "Shit. I've gotta go."

Relief spread across her face. "Running late for work?" she asked.

"Yeah."

"Where?"

"Griffin's," I said.

"Have fun," she said a little curtly.

"Hold on a second," I said, moving toward her.

She stopped and turned around. "What?"

I grinned. "Do you want to get together later?"

Terin snorted. "You're kidding, right?"

"No. Of course not."

She sighed. "Look, I admit, I'm attracted to you but other than that, we have nothing in common."

"We both like to work out," I offered.

"I never said I liked to. I have to."

"Then let me show you a workout you'd enjoy," I said, wiggling my eyebrows.

"Give it up, Johnson. It's not going to happen," she answered, trying not to smile.

"You keep telling yourself that."

Shaking her head, she left the room.

Twenty-three

TERIN

LUCKILY, I FOUND an available treadmill. As I began jogging, I saw Cole leave the weight room and head toward the men's locker area. Some of the other women in the gym watched him leave as well. There was no denying that Cole was one fine specimen of a man. But, he was also dangerous in so many ways. One night with him could potentially get me fired and I wasn't about to take any chances.

My phone began to vibrate again. Sighing, I slowed down and noticed that the person who'd called me earlier, someone who'd obviously had the wrong number, had just sent me a photo. I stopped the treadmill and opened up the message.

What the hell?

It was a picture of me and Cole, in the weight room. Both of us were staring into each other's eyes and it looked much too intimate for comfort.

The phone buzzed again and there was a message from the same number.

Fraternizing with the enemy?

It was the same words the caller had said to me when I'd answered earlier.

Angry, I called the number but nobody answered. I listened to the voicemail.

"You've reached Cole Johnson. Sorry I can't take your call right now. Leave me a message and I'll get back to you as soon as I can."

Cole's phone?

Stunned, I left him a message. "Uh... hi. It's Terin. Could you give me a call as soon as you get this? Thanks."

Still confused, I hung up and went back into the weight room. The other man who'd been working his legs earlier was still inside, doing butterflies. Convinced that he'd somehow gotten Cole's phone and was messing with me, I decided to talk to the asshole.

"Excuse me," I said, walking over to him.

He continued working out. "Yeah?"

"I need to ask you something."

The guy, who I noticed had very light blue eyes and almost a baby face, sighed and stopped doing his reps. "What can I do for you?"

I frowned. His voice sounded very different from the caller's. My gut told me he wasn't the same guy. "Did you happen to find a phone in here?"

"No. Why?"

"My friend that was in here is missing his. Did you happen to see anyone else in here within the last fifteen minutes?"

"No. Just you and your friend." He smiled. "Cole."

"So, you know him?" I asked, curious.

He nodded. "I've done some of his ink, and once in a while, we spot for each other at the gym here."

"Really? He didn't mention that," I replied, wondering if this guy really did have Cole's phone and was messing with me.

"I think he had his mind on other things," replied the guy with a twinkle in his eyes.

"Are you sure that nobody else stopped in here?" I asked, ignoring his comment.

He thought back and then his eyes lit up. "Actually, now that I think about it, some older dude stuck his head in. It was just for a second."

My eyes widened. "Did he say anything to you?"

"No. He was busy checking his phone."

"Checking his phone... Could he have been taking a picture?"

The stranger shrugged. "Yeah. I guess he could have been doing that. Why?"

"Just curious. What did the guy look like?"

"I didn't pay him much attention. The only thing I really noticed was that he was older."

"How old?"

"Fifties. Maybe even sixties."

"Did he have glasses? A beard? Or anything else that you can think of?"

"His face was pock-marked and tan. He had a lot of gray in his hair."

"Heavy-set?"

"I don't know. Like I said, he just stuck his head inside the doorway. Why? What's going on?"

"Nothing. Thank you for the information," I said, sighing. I left the room and went out to the parking lot, hoping that I hadn't missed Cole. When I noticed that his motorcycle was still in the parking lot, I walked back into the building and waited for him outside of the locker room. Ten minutes later, he strolled out, frowning. When he noticed me, his face brightened.

"Hey, what's up?" he asked, stopping next to me.

"Are you missing your cell phone?" I replied, noticing that he'd taken a shower and was now wearing a tight-fitting T-shirt that read *Griffin's.*

He looked surprised. "Yeah. How did you know? Did you find it?"

"No, but the person who apparently has it sent me this," I said, and then showed him the picture.

His face twisted into an angry scowl. "What the fuck?"

"Yeah, I know. Real cute. When was the last time you saw your phone?"

"I'm certain I had it when I arrived. I usually store it in my locker when I'm working out. I noticed that it wasn't there when I went back in to take a shower. I searched the locker room and went back to the gym, but didn't see it."

"Do you use a lock?"

"Yes," he answered. "And it was still locked when I went back there after my workout."

"The person who sent me this photo, using your phone, was the same one who called me when we were in the gym. I spoke to the guy who was in there with us and he mentioned that someone poked their head in and could have taken the picture."

"Quinn? Did he know the guy who took the picture?" asked Cole.

"Doesn't sound like it." I gave him Quinn's description of the man.

"Could have been anyone," said Cole, running a hand quickly through his damp hair.

"Not anyone. Someone who knows us both and is trying to piss me off."

He sighed. "Do you have any idea who it could be?"

Bronson's face popped into my head. He was in his thirties, though, and didn't fit the description. "No. I guess I don't."

Cole swore. "I need my damn phone back. If I get my hands on this guy, he's in deep shit."

"You should call your cell provider and see if they can track it down," I said.

He nodded. "Good idea. I'll have to do that," he replied and then looked toward the front desk. "I should probably check the Lost and Found, too."

"I guess it can't hurt."

"Cole!"

We both turned around and saw Quinn heading toward us. He was holding up a cell phone.

Cole's face lit up. "Sweet. My phone. Where did you find it?"

"It was sitting in the locker room," he replied. "On the bathroom sink."

"How did you know it was his?" I asked, still not too sure about Quinn.

"Easy." He looked at Cole. "I went in and looked at a couple of the texts and pictures. One of them was of your most recent tattoo. Obviously, I recognized it."

"Nothing else like it, brother," said Cole, raising his shirt.

"You did that?" I asked, staring in appreciation at the dragon on Cole's abs.

Quinn nodded.

"Wow. Great work."

"Thank you," he replied. "It took quite a few hours. Ask Cole about it. He cried like a baby."

"Fuck you," said Cole, smiling.

"Okay, he *whined* like a baby," said Quinn.

"I was hangry," said Cole, dropping his shirt. "I should have eaten something before showing up that day. Anyway, Quinn does excellent work. He's my new go-to man."

"Thanks," said Quinn. "You have any ink?"

I shook my head.

"If you ever decide to get one, stop in at Ink Me. I'll do your first one for free."

My eyes widened. "Free?"

"Once you get your first one, it's like an addiction. He knows you'll be back," said Cole, looking through his phone.

"I saw the picture with you two. That's kind of weird, huh?" said Quinn. "It's almost like someone is stalking one of you."

"No shit," said Cole.

"Could it be Patty?" asked Quinn.

"I don't think so," said Cole. "At least I hope not."

"Then it probably was that old man I noticed in the gym. Did you tell Cole about him?" asked Quinn.

"Yes," I replied.

"You ever see him here before?" asked Cole.

"No, but then I don't pay too much attention to other guys," said Quinn. "When I'm here, I'm pretty focused on my workout. Or chicks."

"I hear you," said Cole.

"I have to get going. Good luck with the stalker. If I see him around, I'll let you know," said Quinn.

"Thanks, man," said Cole.

Quinn looked at me. "Nice meeting you...?"

"Terin," I said. "Nice meeting you too, Quinn."

"Don't forget... Ink Me. We just opened up in downtown Jensen. Tell your friends and neighbors."

"I won't forget," I said, amused.

"And... if you want your cherry popped," he said, winking, "I'm your man."

I raised my eyebrow. "Come again?"

Cole laughed.

"You have virgin skin," explained Quinn, smiling.

"Ah. So have you popped a lot of cherries?" I asked, thinking that he probably had a lot of young women standing in line to be tattooed.

"I've had my share. Don't worry, I'm very gentle. At least when I can be," he added.

"I'll keep that in mind," I replied.

"Good luck catching the creepy old geezer," said Quinn. "And I'll see you around Cole."

"Definitely."

"So, did the asshole do anything to your phone?" I asked Cole, after Quinn left us.

"Doesn't appear like it," he said, scowling.

I nodded toward his phone. "You have anything in there that could get you into trouble?"

"Besides the picture of you and me?" he said, smiling. "No."

"Could you please erase it?"

"Why?" he asked, pulling the photo up. "It's a good picture."

I had to agree but that wasn't the point. "Some creepoid took it."

Cole's smile faded. "True." He put his finger on the 'Delete' button. "If I erase it, will you let me take another one of you?"

I tilted my head. "Why do you need a picture of me?" I asked dryly.

"So I can assign it as your contact picture," he said innocently. "I wouldn't want to forget what you looked like."

I snorted.

"I'm serious. If you want me to delete it, then I need another."

"Fine," I huffed.

Smiling, he held his phone up. "Smile."

I did.

"Beautiful. What would make it even better is if you," Cole gave me a wicked smile, "raised your shirt."

I raised my middle finger instead.

He laughed and took the picture.

Twenty-four

COLE

AFTER WALKING OUT of the gym, I called Tank from the parking lot and told him about the incident.

"That's fucked up. Someone is messing with the both of you."

"Apparently."

"It has to be someone from the Devil's Rangers," he added. "Could even be the same person who called in the 'anonymous' tip."

"I was thinking that myself."

"You on your way to Griffin's?"

"Yes. Obviously, I'm going to be a few minutes late."

"That's fine. Have a good night."

"You're not going to be there?"

"No. Raina has to work late and I'm watching Billy. We just got done bringing her dinner."

"How's he doing?"

"Great. He's such a good kid. Frannie just adores him. So do I."

"He's easy to love," I answered.

"He sure is. Oh, I have to go. He needs help brushing his teeth before hitting the hay."

"Tell him I love him, will you?"

"I will."

After hanging up with Tank, I jumped on my bike and headed to work, still wondering who the fuck had taken my phone. And even stranger, why did they bother to return it?

Twenty-five

TERIN

I DIDN'T FEEL like working out anymore so I grabbed my stuff, went home, and drew myself a hot bath. As the water ran, I took out my phone to look at the picture again. I had to admit, it was a good photo of the two of us. Especially of him. The man was dangerously sexy.

Sighing, I went into the kitchen, poured myself a glass of wine, and brought into the bathroom with me. Then I lowered myself into the tub, had a few sips of wine, and closed my eyes, imagining Cole's hand on my thigh and then other more intimate places.

After my bath, I filled my vibrator with batteries and eventually fell asleep with a smile on my face.

***

When my alarm went off the next morning, it felt as if I'd just closed my eyes. Yawning, I went into the kitchen, brewed a cup of coffee, and turned on the television.

"Two bodies were discovered just after three a.m. near Center Lake. Officials have not yet released the identities of the two victims, but foul play is suspected."

My cell phone rang. It was Walters.

194

"Hello," I said, still staring at the television, which was now showing images of the lake and area where the bodies had been found.

"You see the news?" asked Walters.

"I'm watching it right now. Do we have any idea of who the victims were?"

"Yep. The same two we've been looking for. Ronnie and Pete."

My jaw dropped. "You're kidding? Both of them?"

"Yes."

"How did they die?"

"Pete was shot in the head and Ronnie was strangled."

"Were they killed at the same time?"

"Annie in Forensics believes that Pete was killed several hours before Ronnie."

"So, Ronnie probably killed him and then someone decided to off Ronnie?"

"Yeah. That's what I'm thinking. Both were found in a stolen older model Chevy Impala. Pete was in the trunk and Ronnie was found in the driver's seat."

"Oh wow."

"It gets better," he said, a smile in his voice.

"What do you mean?"

"There was evidence found about ten feet from the vehicle."

"What did they find?"

"A business card for Griffin's. Written on the back was the name Cole Johnson."

Twenty-six

COLE

I **WOKE UP** to the sound of someone pounding on my front door. I looked at the clock and it was nine a.m. It had been a late night and I was still tired as all hell.

Grumbling to myself, I got out of bed, pulled on a pair of jeans, and headed downstairs to see who the fuck was disturbing me. It definitely wasn't who I'd expected.

"Terin. I mean, Detective... what are you doing here?" I asked, rubbing my eye.

"I tried calling you but you didn't answer your phone," she said, staring at me.

"Sorry. It's probably in my kitchen. I was still sleeping," I answered, reaching into my pocket. I pulled out a pack of mint gum and took a piece.

"Late night?" she asked, watching me shove it into my mouth.

"Yeah. You could say that. Do you want a piece of gum?"

"I'm good."

"What about coffee? I can make some."

She nodded. "Sure."

I stepped aside and she walked into the foyer.

"Nice place."

198

"I'm just renting it," I told her, shutting the door. It was a newer townhouse and the landlady, a cougar who lived next door, had given me a great deal on the place. One, because she had the hots for me, and two, because I agreed to mow the lawn and shovel snow during the winter. She'd hit on me a couple of times and once even showed up at my door wearing a miniscule bikini. The problem was that she was married and I didn't fuck anyone with a ring on their finger, no matter how tempting the offering.

She followed me into the kitchen.

"You working right now?" I asked, noticing that she was dressed in gray slacks and a white blouse.

"I'm on my way there."

"How do you like your coffee?" I asked, starting the coffee machine.

"Do you have any cream or sugar?"

"I've got some almond milk and sugar."

Her face brightened. "You drink almond milk?"

"I'm lactose intolerant," I told her. "Plus, I like it."

"I'll have some, if that's okay? And, don't worry about the sugar."

"Okay." I walked over to the refrigerator. "So, what's going on? Did you figure out who took my phone last night?"

"Nope. I did not and I take it you didn't either?"

"No. It really pisses me off, too. I almost want to get a new phone, knowing that someone was tampering with mine."

"I probably would myself," she answered. "Anyway, speaking of last night, what time did you work until?"

"The bar closed at two. I helped clean up and then went home. Why?"

"Did you stop anywhere else?"

"No." I frowned. "What's this about?"

"You have people who can vouch for you?"

I didn't like her tone or the way she was looking at me. Like I was the enemy. "Yeah, why?"

"Because someone murdered Ronnie last night and there was a business card with your name written on it, just a few feet away."

I stared at her in shock. "You're kidding me? Ronnie's dead?"

She nodded. "You weren't aware of this?"

"No, of course not. Did they find Pete?"

"Yes. They found him in the trunk of a car. One that Ronnie apparently stole."

"Wait a second... you're here because you think that I had something to do with it?"

"Did you?"

I scowled. "No. Of course not," I said sharply. "Do you really think I'm a murderer?"

"I would like to think that you're not," she said, studying my face. "But, the kind of people you mix with are, and I'm pretty sure you know that."

"And you have proof that my club brothers are murderers?" I barked.

"Look, I'm just trying to do my job here," she replied.

I walked over to her. "And not doing very well at it, apparently. You know, just because they found a card with my name written on it doesn't mean I'm a fucking murderer," I snapped.

Twenty-seven

TERIN

HE WAS ANGRIER than all hell and part of me couldn't blame him. That is... if he was innocent. I wanted to believe that Cole was, but I really didn't know him or what he was capable of.

"Okay. So, it's not you," I said, staring up at him. "Could it be another member of the Gold Vipers? I mean, it makes the most sense, right?"

"If it was one of them, I'd know," said Cole.

"But, obviously you wouldn't tell me, right?"

His eyes grew stormy.

"It's an honest question. I mean, isn't that how clubs like this operate? You make your own rules and fuck everyone else?"

He still didn't say anything, which started to really piss *me* off.

"Are you going to answer my questions, or do I need to bring you in?"

Cole laughed coldly. "Bring me in for what? There's no proof that I killed anyone. I have an alibi. And there is obviously no weapon linking me to the scene."

"How do you know they didn't find a weapon?"

"Because if they did and my fingerprints were on it, there'd be more than just you here right now."

"If I wanted to take you in, I could do it without any help," I snapped.

"Just like you did with Chips?" he asked, smiling cruelly.

I clenched my jaw. "Fuck you."

He spit his gum out into the garbage can. "If you say so, Detective."

I thought I'd heard him incorrectly but then he grabbed my arms and pulled me against his chest. Crushing his lips against mine, he forced my mouth open with his tongue, thrusting it inside of me. Overcome with my own pent-up lust, I slid my hands around his neck and began kissing him back, my body aching with desire. The vibrator had taken the edge off last night, but it could never replace the touch of a real man, which I needed badly.

Growling in the back of his throat, Cole's hands went to my blouse. He squeezed and fondled my breasts through the fabric. Before I knew it, the buttons were undone and he was yanking my bra above my nipples, too impatient to unclasp it. Picking me up, he set me down on the center island and brought my nipples to his mouth, first one and then the other. As he sucked and rolled the hard nubs with his tongue, I wrapped my legs around his hips and threw my head back, moaning in pleasure.

"I've got your weapon right here, Detective," he growled, rubbing his pelvis against mine. "You sure you want it?"

A rush of tingling, tightening desire twisted along my spine, hitting me in the crotch. "Yes," I gasped as he began humping me through his jeans. I wanted him deep and I wanted him hard.

Kissing my lips again, Cole unbuttoned my pants and pulled them away from my hips. When they were on the floor, he slid his finger under my panties, to my slit.

Gasping, I dug my fingernails into his bare back as need wrenched through me.

"Terin," he whispered into my ear. "God, I'm going to come just touching you like this."

I moaned again as his rough fingers began rubbing up and down my clit.

"I need to taste you. In fact, I'm going to make you come so hard, you're going to beg to have me fuck you," he said, ripping my panties away. The next thing I knew, his face was between my thighs and his tongue found my clit, making me lose my mind. Then he plunged his finger inside of me while teasing me with his mouth until I was screaming out an orgasm.

Gasping and trying to catch my breath, I next found myself being picked up and carried upstairs to his bedroom. He tossed me onto his mattress and pulled off his belt.

"What are you going to do with that?" I asked, noticing that he was coming toward me with it.

He grinned wickedly. "Don't worry. I won't hurt you. Unless you want me to."

I swallowed.

Cole took his belt and tied my wrists to the metal headboard. He then removed my blouse and bra, until I was totally nude.

"Detective, you're fucking beautiful," he said, stepping back. "I should take a picture of you like this."

"You do and I'll kill you."

He unbuttoned his jeans. "You don't look like you're in any kind of position to be making threats."

"Try me," I said huskily, as he pulled his jeans down, revealing his cock, which was hard, red, and pulsating.

"Oh, I'm planning on it," he said, crawling toward me on the bed. Cole wrapped his hand around his manhood and brought it near my lips.

"Are you really just going to stand there?" I whispered, thinking that I'd never seen one so perfect. My womanhood ached to feel it inside of me.

He stroked his cock a couple of times, right above my mouth. "The truth is, I just realized that I don't have any rubbers," he confessed. "And I want you so fucking bad."

"You're serious?"

"I've been meaning to pick some up," he said, fondling my breast with the other hand. "You wouldn't happen to have one with you?"

I laughed. "Right. No. I don't carry rubbers with me. Especially on the job."

"I had to ask."

"It's been months since I've had sex and even then, I didn't carry any with me."

"It's been months?"

"Yes."

"So, you're going to be pretty tight," he replied huskily, moving his hand between my legs again.

I closed my eyes and moaned as he slipped two fingers between my legs. He leaned over me and began teasing my nipples again.

"Wait. You need to come. Fuck my breasts," I panted.

Cole got onto the bed and straddled me. He grabbed ahold of my breasts and slid his cock between them. Crushing my boobs against his shaft, he moved his hips back and forth, fucking my cleavage. It didn't take long before his breathing became ragged.

"Fuck," he gasped, stiffening up. Holding my breasts tightly, he came violently, his face twisting in pleasure. When it was over, he gave me a sheepish grin. "Sorry, let me clean you up."

"It's quite all right."

He went into the bathroom and came out a short time later with a damp towel.

"Guess what?" he said, walking toward me. He gave me a sheepish smile. "I found a condom in my medicine cabinet."

I scowled at him. "Seriously?"

He chuckled. "Don't worry. I'll be ready to go in five minutes. I'm younger than you, remember?"

Not only that, but my conscience had returned and I knew that I'd made a mistake. "Cole, unbuckle me."

"Hold on. Let's get you cleaned off first," he said, wiping his seed off with the towel.

"Thanks."

"My pleasure."

When he was finished, he dropped the towel but made no move to free me.

"Well?" I asked, nodding toward the belt. "What are you waiting for? Unbuckle this."

He placed his finger next to my bellybutton and began making circles around it.

"Cole."

He smirked. "Maybe I should just keep you here all day."

"You only have one condom," I reminded him.

His finger moved down to my slit. "I don't need one for my tongue," he whispered.

I moaned as Cole began pleasuring me down below again, first with his fingers and then his lips. Because he had me at such a vulnerable position, and was beginning to know what I liked, I came even harder than the previous time.

Cole sat up, wiping his mouth with the back of his hand. "*Now*, I'm going to fuck your brains out," he said, ripping open the condom. He rolled it over his cock and then moved between my legs. Grabbing my hips, he positioned us both and then plunged inside. We both gasped in pleasure at the tight fit.

"Damn," he whispered.

"Damn is right. Keep going," I said breathlessly.

Cole pulled out half way and then thrust into me again.

"Faster and harder," I demanded.

"You like to give orders, don't you?" he growled near my ear.

"When it feels this good, yes," I answered, biting him playfully on his shoulder.

Cole began fucking me fast and hard, just like I'd asked. After a few minutes, he took off the belt and I got on top, riding him until we both came at the same time. When we were both spent and sweaty, he dragged me into the shower with him.

"You know... we can't tell anyone about this," I said, staring at the wall. "I could get fired."

"I won't say anything," he said. "You have my word."

Sighing, I closed my eyes as his fingers slid through my hair and he began washing it.

"Feel good?" he asked, massaging my scalp.

"Yes," I said. "Everything you've done to me so far feels really good."

"I'm not done with you yet," he said, pulling me back against his chest. I could feel his penis rubbing against my backside and decided that maybe I would take Walters up on his offer of letting me have the day off.

MEANWHILE,

IN

VEGAS

Twenty-eight

JESSICA

AS USUAL, I woke up alone in the master bedroom of the house we were renting in Vegas, feeling both frustrated and angry with Jordan. We'd been there for three weeks and I'd barely seen him the last two. Although he claimed that he was tying up loose ends and working on making a future for us, I couldn't understand why it had to take up so much of his time. Most days, he was gone for eight to ten hours. Then we'd have dinner and sex. There was barely enough time to talk and that was hard enough to get him to do.

I stood up, put on a robe, and headed out of the bedroom and into the gourmet kitchen, which was on the other side of the house. It was a basically a mansion, about six thousand square feet and more than the two of us needed. The only reason we were renting it was because Jordan knew the owner and trusted him. Still, it was enormous and I couldn't help but feel somewhat lost in it. Especially since I was alone most of the time. In fact, I was lonely and so damn bored that I almost couldn't wait to get back to Jensen. Sure, Jordan had rented a car for me to use and had given me money for sightseeing, but there was no fun in doing it alone. And, I couldn't even complain, since he'd warned me in advance that he wouldn't be around much.

Sighing, I stepped into the kitchen and noticed that he'd sent over yet another bouquet of fresh flowers. It wasn't that I didn't appreciate the gesture, it's that I just knew that he was sending them because he felt guilty. There were now six vases sitting in the kitchen, each filled with everything from roses to daisies.

At least the kitchen smells lovely, I thought.

Wondering what the excuse would be this time, I opened the note and read the card.

I'm going to be gone until late.
I'm so sorry and promise to make it up to you.
Love,
Jordan

Gritting my teeth, I crumpled up the note and threw it into the garbage. We only had four more days left in Vegas and it didn't look like he was going to make good on the promise of driving out to Lake Tahoe. It was a half day trip and we were supposed to spend time there before returning to Iowa.

"Dammit, Jordan," I muttered, my eyes filling with frustrated tears.

"Good morning, Miss Jessica."

Trying to compose myself, I turned around and forced a smile to my lips. It was the housekeeper-slash-cook who Jordan had hired for our stay. "Good morning, Maria."

Maria, who spoke very little English, but had been the kindest person to me since we'd arrived in Vegas, must have noticed that I was upset. She walked over to me and touched my arm. "Are you... okay?"

"I'm fine," I told her.

She stared at my eyes and I knew she didn't believe me. But, Maria didn't press anything. "Hungry?" she asked.

"I'll just make myself a piece of toast," I told her, walking over to the refrigerator.

"I'll get it," she said, following me. "You... sit."

"No, it's okay. I can do it," I told her.

"It's my job," she said. It was something she'd been repeating quite a bit the last three weeks. I'd learned from Jordan that Maria was getting paid well and wanted to earn her keep.

"Don't get in her way," he'd said. "When she says she wants to do something, I've learned to let her do it."

"So, you've used her before?" I'd asked.

"Just a couple of times. She's a friend of my sister. She's also very stubborn"

I moved out of Maria's way. "Okay. If you insist."

Smiling, Maria started humming to herself as she made me toast.

"Butter and jam?" she asked.

"Just butter," I replied, sitting down at the counter. "Please."

When she was done, there was toast along with fruit, and vanilla yogurt sitting in front of me.

215

"For baby," she said, nodding toward the other two items. "Eat."

I gave her a puzzled look.

She smiled and patted her stomach.

"Oh. I'm not pregnant," I told her, not knowing if I should laugh or feel insulted. Even though I'd gained a couple of pounds, it wasn't because I was pregnant. It was from being bored and stuffing my face. In fact, I knew for sure that I wasn't. I'd taken a pregnancy test a couple of weeks ago and it had been negative.

"Yes. A girl," she said and then gave me a horrified look. "I'm sorry, Miss Jessica."

I snorted. "Sorry? For what?"

"My big... mouth," she said in broken English. "Maybe boy?"

"I'm telling you, I'm not pregnant so it's okay."

She bit her lip and nodded. "Okay. You eat, though."

I raised the toast to my lips and took a bite. "There, are you happy?" I asked, my mouth full.

She smiled and went over to the refrigerator. I ate silently and watched as she poured me a glass of milk. Maria brought it over and set it down.

"Let me guess," I said wryly. "It's good for the baby?"

Maria nodded.

Smiling in amusement, I thanked her for the breakfast.

"You're welcome," she replied and then left me alone.

When I was finished, I went back to the bedroom and put my bathing suit on. Then I headed outside to the pool, taking along with me a book that I'd been reading, and sunscreen. Settling in on one of the lawn chairs, I sprayed myself with the sunscreen and opened up the book.

"You forgot this," said Maria, appearing next to me and holding my cell phone.

I looked up and smiled. "Thank you for bringing it out to me."

She handed it to me. "Be careful. Hot today."

"Today? It's hot here every day," I replied, setting my book down. "Thank goodness for the pool."

"Oh yes. My niños love to swim."

"Your children?"

She nodded.

I stared at the pool, which was a good size and even had a slide. "Well then, invite them over to swim."

"No," she said, looking embarrassed.

"Nonsense. I'd love to meet your kids and I'm bored as all hell. Invite them over. Please."

She gave me a doubtful look.

"Maria, I'm serious. We have this amazing swimming pool and it's being wasted. Please, bring them here so I can have some fun."

"Fun?"

"Yes," I said smiling. "Watching them play is going to be a lot of fun. At least for me. How many children do you have?"

"Four," she replied.

"Well, go and round them up. Bring them here," I demanded.

"You sure?"

"I've never been so sure in my life."

An hour later, Maria's children were splashing and playing in the pool. There were three girls, ranging from eight to sixteen, and one boy, who I guessed to be ten.

"Will you swim with us?" asked the youngest girl.

I put my book down and stood up. "I'd love to," I said, smiling down at her. Her name was Sofia and she had long, dark hair and big brown eyes, just like her mother.

Sofia smiled back.

I got in and we played a game of Marco Polo along with some other games. After a short time, I was laughing and enjoying myself so much, that we all lost track of time. Soon it was the afternoon and the children had to leave.

"It was so nice having you over," I told them as they gathered their towels and sandals. "All of you. I hope you can come back again?"

"Us too," said Sofia, throwing her arms around my waist.

Smiling I hugged her back, wishing that Maria had been right and that I was pregnant.

"I mean it," I told Maria, as she pulled out her car keys. "Bring them back in the next couple of days. We had so much fun together."

Maria smiled at me and said something in Spanish.

"What was that?" I asked.

"She said that you will be a good mother," explained Sofia.

I laughed. She just wouldn't give up. "Thank you, Maria. Someday."

"Soon," said the housekeeper, a twinkle in her eyes. "Someday soon."

Twenty-nine

JORDAN

"IT'S DONE," I said into the phone.

"And how do I know this?" asked the voice.

"Watch the news tonight," I replied.

She sighed. "Thank you."

"You can do so by getting me that passport and driver's license."

"It's ready. So is the social security number."

I sighed in relief. "So, there's nothing fishy about the new ID? It's legit?"

"You're damn right and I worked very hard to pull this one off. Just like I knew you'd do the same for me."

I thought of the man I'd murdered an hour before. He owned a casino and was one of the biggest crooks in Vegas. Needless to say, his security had been tight. So tight that it had taken me almost two weeks to get close enough to the mafia man and earn both his interest and trust. It had been one of my most challenging jobs, especially since I'd had to play the part of a gay card dealer. Fortunately for me, there'd been no kissing involved, but Alessandro Giovanni had certainly gotten fucked. Just not in the way he'd anticipated.

"You still have the P.O. box to send everything to?" I asked Alessandro's wife. A woman who he used to beat so badly that she now walked with a permanent limp. I had no qualms about ending his miserable life. I'd just given her back hers.

"I do. Is he really gone?" she asked in a shaky voice.

"He'll never harm you again. I give you my word."

She thanked me and began to cry.

Thirty

JESSICA

I T WAS JUST past seven. Another uneventful evening of eating dinner alone. Bored out of my mind, and a little pissed off, I decided to do something spontaneous and... a little bad. I put on a sexy black dress and drove to Bally's on the Vegas strip. I used their valet parking and went inside to gamble away some of Jordan's money.

Unfortunately, unlike most of the gamblers in Vegas, I couldn't seem to lose. It was almost humorous.

"You're kidding?!" I squealed, winning another hand of Blackjack.

"Nope. You just won five thousand dollars," said the dealer, sliding over my chips. "Are you sure you've never played this before?"

"Just with my family," I replied, stacking my chips. "I usually never win with them though."

After a few more rounds and winnings, I noticed a crowd gathering around me.

"How much are you up, doll?" asked a burly man wearing a black suit. He reminded me of a bouncer and I wondered if maybe I was winning too much and I was in trouble.

"I think she must be up about one-hundred grand," said one of the other players.

"That's incredible," he said. "How many hands did it take to win all of that?"

"Uh, I don't know. I've been here for about an hour, I think," I replied, giving the other player a dirty look.

The dealer, a woman about my age, nodded toward the clock. "Actually, it's been more like two."

"I should take my winnings and quit while I'm ahead," I answered, laughing nervously. "You know, unlike those people in the movies. The ones who keep playing until they lose it all?"

"Sometimes it's better to quit while you're ahead," said a person standing on the other side of me. "If I were you, I'd try another hand though."

I turned and noticed that the man was blind.

"You think I should play another round?" I asked, biting my lower lip. I wanted to but something inside of me screamed to take my winnings and leave.

The stranger, who had dark skin, dreadlocks, and kind of reminded me of Stevie Wonder, grinned. "Sure. Why not? You're in Vegas. You're having a good time, and you're ahead."

"Okay. I'll play one more and that's it. You're not going to tell me to go all or nothing, are you?" I asked, amused.

The man grinned. "Never go all in unless you have a backup plan. Take it from me."

Something in his voice gave him away.

Jordan Steele, you crafty little devil.

I wasn't sure how he found me, but apparently he was up to his old tricks again. His disguise was good, but I was better.

"I agree. Having a backup plan is always a good thing," I replied. "But so is having common sense. I'm going to take my winnings and get a room."

Jordan's smile faltered.

"Here," I said to the dealer, handing her about ten thousand dollars in chips. "A tip."

"Thanks," she said, smiling widely.

Wanting to flirt with Jordan while he was in his disguise, but not wanting him to catch on that I'd made him, I asked the dealer how much the suites cost in the hotel.

"I'm not sure," she replied.

"Are you staying here?" asked Jordan.

"Yes."

"Alone?"

"You know, my mother told me not to talk to strangers, especially in Vegas," I replied, smiling.

He smiled back. "Wise woman."

"The thing is, being wise can be very boring," I said. "Which is what it's been like for me the past few days. So… tonight, I think I'm going to have me a 'what happens in Vegas, stays in Vegas,' kinds of night."

He didn't say anything.

I hid my grin. "Well, everyone, have a good night. I know I am," I said.

The other players wished me well.

I thanked them and walked away from the table.

From there, I cashed in my chips and checked into an expensive suite. Although I couldn't see Jordan, I knew he was around and watching me like a hawk.

Smiling to myself, I took the elevator up to the room I'd reserved, ordered a bottle of champagne, and kicked off my shoes. Once the concierge delivered the bottle, I drew myself a bath, poured myself a glass of champagne, and got into the tub.

It wasn't long before my cell phone went off. I reached over and grabbed it.

Jordan : *Miss me?*

Me: *What do you think?*

Jordan: *I should be home soon.*

Me: *Good for you.*

Jordan: *Angry?*

Me: *Frustrated.*

Jordan: *I can tell. Let me do something about that.*

I heard the click of the bathroom door and Jordan walked in.

"Surprised that I found you here?" he asked, walking over to the bathtub. He'd changed out of his disguise and was now wearing a pair of black trousers and a white dress shirt open at the collar.

I took a sip of my champagne and smiled. "No. I'm just surprised that it took you this long to find my room."

He began unbuttoning his shirt. "How did you happen to know that it was me down there?"

"I guess I just know when the man I love is standing next to me," I replied, watching as he undressed. "Especially when he's never around." My eyes filled with tears.

He took off his pants and got into the tub with me. "Jessica," he said, cupping my face with his hands. He stared into my eyes. "I'm here."

"Are you?" I asked, staring into his ice blue eyes.

"Yes," he said. "And I'm never leaving you again. I promise."

"What about tomorrow?" I asked, hating the way my throat was closing up and how emotional he made me. "Will there be flowers and maybe another note, apologizing that you had to leave again?"

"Tomorrow? Just flowers. You can't have a wedding without them."

I stared at him in confusion.

He grinned. "You still want to get married, don't you?"

"To you?" I asked, the tears running down my cheeks.

"That's the idea."

Crying, I threw my arms around his neck and cried, "Yes!"

"There is one little issue."

I stiffened up. Another catch? "What's that?" I asked pulling away.

"You're not going to be Jessica Steele. You're going to be Jessica Stone. That is, if you'd like to take my new last name."

"I'm okay with that," I replied, relieved that it was something so trivial. "What about your first name? You didn't change that, did you?"

"No. It's Jordan."

"Phew. I don't know if I could have lived with a first name change," I teased. "Last name, that's fine. First name... absolutely not."

Jordan grinned. "Just don't call me 'Judge'," he said. "That chapter in my life is finally closed."

"For good?"

"For good."

I smiled. "So, how should we begin this new chapter?"

"I have a suggestion," he said, touching me intimately.

We started the chapter with sex. Lots and lots of it.

MEANWHILE,

BACK IN

JENSEN...

Thirty-one

TERIN

AFTER COLE AND I stepped out of the shower, he went into the kitchen to make us something to eat while I checked in with Walters.

"Did you talk to Cole Johnson?" he asked.

"Yes," I said, lowering my voice.

"What did he say?"

"He was shocked and claimed he didn't know anything about Ronnie and Pete. He also has an alibi for last night."

"What's the alibi?"

"He was working at Griffin's."

Walters sighed. "Even without one, I'm sure he didn't do it. Someone wanted us to find that card so we'd divert our attention to Cole. Besides, who carries around a business card with one's own name written on the back?"

"True."

"Someone is trying to frame him."

"The same person who called in the tip yesterday?"

"Maybe, although we thought it was the Devil's Rangers and now one of them is dead."

"Would one of the Devil's Rangers kill their own V.P. just to frame Cole?"

"Yes, if there's more going on than we know. These clubs act like it's all about the brotherhood and trusting each other, but that only goes so far. Especially when you're dealing with a club like the Devil's Rangers."

"So, you think it was an inside job?"

"Sure. If someone higher up than Ronnie ordered one of the club members to take him out, I bet the person wouldn't blink an eye. It would just happen."

"Do you think Schmitty could have ordered it?"

"It's possible. Look at the mess Ronnie's created while Schmitty's been on his road trip. Not to mention, being out of town is also a good alibi for the club president."

He had an excellent point.

"I know these clubs. I've been following them for years and have learned to never rule anything out. Especially inside jobs."

"So, what's the next step?"

"I'm waiting to see if we can identify who was on the video footage and if they get any prints or DNA from the crime scene, other than what's expected."

"Okay."

"I'll let you know if we find out anything. Meanwhile, enjoy your day off and we'll see you bright and early tomorrow."

"Sounds good."

After ending the call, I walked into the kitchen wearing one of Cole's T-shirts, and found him making ham and cheese omelets.

"Those look delicious," I said, peeking around his shoulder.

"Thank you. Why don't you make yourself at home and I'll fix you a plate?"

I went and sat down at the kitchen table while Cole finished the eggs. His home and his kitchen was nicer than mine and I wondered where his money came from.

"You're quiet," he said, bringing the plates over.

"I was just thinking," I answered, staring down at the food. "You know, I don't think I've ever had a man make me breakfast before. Thank you."

"You're welcome." He nodded toward the clock. "It's more like lunch, but I can eat eggs any time of the day."

"Me, too."

We began eating and I had to admit, the silence was a little awkward. He noticed it too.

"So, are you thinking again?" he asked, looking at me.

I took a sip of coffee. "I'm always thinking."

"Don't think too hard. It'll stress you out."

"Easier said than done," I replied. "So, tell me more about yourself, Cole Johnson. And I'm not talking about club stuff."

He grinned. "What do you want to know?"

"What are your hopes and dreams?"

Cole laughed. "Right now? I'm hoping to get my hands on some condoms so that I'm able to dream with a smile on my face tonight."

I smirked. "What makes you think we'll be having sex again?"

"You're still here, aren't you?"

"I'm hungry."

He gave me a devilish grin. "So am I."

Thirty-two

COLE

AFTER BREAKFAST, I talked Terin into taking a ride on the back of my bike. She put her clothing back on and we cruised around for a couple of hours.

"Did you want to stop by your place and change out of your work-clothes?" I asked her, after stopping at a drug store.

"No, that's okay."

"Are you sure? You'd be more comfortable."

"I'm fine," she answered.

I had a feeling that she didn't want me knowing where she lived. I didn't say anything, but it annoyed me. Especially after the last several hours.

We got back onto my Hog and I asked if she was enjoying herself.

She smiled. "I forgot how much fun it is to be on one of these things. How hard is it drive?"

"Drive? Hell, they're easy to drive. It's the other people on the road that make things difficult. You have to try and anticipate everyone's moves and hope they're paying attention so you don't die."

"I can imagine."

"But, if you're interested in learning, I definitely wouldn't let the other idiots on the road stop you. They have courses you can take and they're only around ten hours to complete. So, you should be able to fit them into your busy schedule."

"What about a motorcycle?"

"They provide you with one of those as well."

She put on the extra brain bucket I'd loaned her. "I'm going to have to check it out."

"Really?"

"Yeah."

"Cool. Then we can go riding together once you learn."

Terin just smiled.

On the way back to my place, we stopped at the grocery store and picked up a couple of ribeye steaks, two potatoes, mushrooms, and a bag of salad.

"Don't you have to work tonight?" she asked me.

"No."

"Is that the only place you work? Griffin's?"

"Nope. I work part-time at Black Diamond Restoration. It's an auto body shop."

"Really? I had no idea," she answered. "What do you do there?"

"I'm one of the paint technicians."

"How long have you worked there for?"

"About three years now."

"Interesting. Do you like it?"

"Yeah. I'd like to be able to put in more hours, but I've been so busy with the club."

"When are they going to patch you?" she asked.

"I don't know. I haven't been with them long, so it might be a while."

"But, you're going to be Tank's brother-in-law soon, right?"

"Yes, but you have to earn your way into the club. Gain everyone's trust," I said.

"You say that like it's not an easy task."

I just shrugged and put my helmet back on. "Nothing is ever easy. Are you ready?"

"Yes." She slid her arms around my waist and we headed back to my place. Once there, we put the groceries away, marinated the steaks, and made use of some of the condoms. Afterward, I fired up the grill and we made dinner together.

"I'm glad you have a healthy appetite," I said, watching her eat. We were sitting outside, having dinner on the patio. "And aren't one of those girls who eats nothing but salad or brown rice."

"To be honest, I don't eat like this all the time. Although, I enjoy it. My schedule is so crazy though and so I eat a lot of fast food."

"I do too, but it's nice to sit down and share a meal like this with someone. We'll have to do this again."

She didn't reply.

"I don't know about you, but I've had a hell of a good time today," I replied, cutting into my steak. "And could get use to this."

"You realize that I'm not supposed to be here," she said softly. "I could get fired."

"Not if you don't get caught."

Terin didn't say anything.

My phone began to ring. It was Tank.

I sighed. "I need to take this. I'll be right back," I said standing up.

"Sure."

"I got your message about Ronnie and Pete, earlier. Sorry it took so long to get back to you," said Tank.

"It's not a problem," I told him. "You have any ideas about who might have done it?"

"No. Wasn't one of us," he said. "Unless you went vigilante and took care of business yourself."

"Hell no."

"Raina was with me all night, so I know she didn't do it," Tank said, sounding amused.

I smiled.

"Had a detective drop by, about twenty minutes ago. This prick named Bronson."

"What did he want?"

"He was trying to find out if we knew anything about Ronnie's murder and then he started asking some questions about you and Detective Terin O'Brien."

I clenched my jaw. "Like what?"

"Personal ones. I think he was trying to find out if you two had something going on."

My thoughts returned to the gym and our stalker. I wondered if the person had sent something to the police. I swore.

"You thinking about that guy who had your phone?"

"Yeah," I replied. "He might be trying to get her fired."

"Did you check your phone to see if he sent the photo to anyone else?"

"Hell yeah I did but it looks like he just sent it to Terin."

"He might have used his own phone to take another picture."

"True."

"Is something going on between you and the cop?" asked Tank.

"Just sex," I admitted.

"So you did bang her." Tank laughed. "Nothing wrong with that."

"Is that all he wanted?"

"I guess Hoss talked to him about some shit, too."

"About what?"

"He told me that he was discussing Facebook and internet scams with the guy and asking for advice. I don't think Bronson was able to help him out with anything though. He looked just as confused as Hoss."

"The old man just needs to stay off social media," I replied.

"No shit. So, are you at work right now?"

"The shop? No, not today."

"You're welcome to stop by tonight. Raina and I are making burgers on the grill."

"I'm actually in the middle of dinner."

"Oh, shit. Sorry. I'll let you go."

"It's fine. You need me for anything tonight or tomorrow?"

"Not tonight. Why don't you check in at the clubhouse around ten a.m.?"

"Will do."

"Later, brother."

"Later," I said and then hung up. I walked back outside and sat down. "Sorry about that."

"Who was it?"

"Tank," I replied. "Looks like someone named Bronson was asking him questions, earlier."

"Bronson? About Ronnie and Pete?"

"Yeah and about us."

"What?" she said sharply.

"He asked Tank if you and I were seeing each other."

She set her fork down. "Dammit. That nosy sonofabitch."

"Do you think he might be the one who took the picture at the gym?"

"No, but I wonder if it's someone Bronson might know though," said Terin, standing up. "I'm sorry, Cole. I'd better get out of here."

"Hold up," I said, pushing my chair back.

"This was a mistake," she answered, her eyes filling with fear. "I don't know what the hell I was thinking."

I walked over and put my hands on her shoulders. "Terin. It's okay. Just, calm down."

"Easy for you to say," she replied. "You're not in danger of losing everything you've worked for."

I pulled her into my arms and held her. "You're not going to lose anything. Even if they found out about us, what could they do? It's not like we're doing anything illegal."

"I'm not supposed to be sleeping with one of the men I'm investigating," she said, pulling away.

"I don't recall us sleeping at all," I teased.

"Not funny," she said, heading into the house.

I followed her. "Are you seriously leaving?"

Terin grabbed her purse and walked quickly toward the front door. "Yes. I'm sorry. I have to get to get the hell out of here. For all I know, they've got someone watching your house and I'm already screwed."

"Terin… wait."

Without another word, she hurried out of the house, got into her car, and sped away.

I thought about going after her, but knew there was nothing that I could say that would change her mind. Not only that, I knew she was right. As much as I wanted to get to know her more, I was the last thing she needed in her life.

Thirty-three

TERIN

KNOWING THAT BRONSON was sticking his nose where it didn't belong made me livid. I wanted to drive to the precinct and threaten him with the tape I'd made, but instead I talked myself down and went home instead. When I arrived, I took a shower to try and calm down, got into a white terrycloth robe, and sat down on the sofa to think things through. As I closed my eyes, the doorbell rang. Wondering if it might be my sister or mother, I stood back up and looked through the peephole.

It was Bronson.

"What in the hell do you want?" I asked sharply, swinging the door open.

Bronson's eyes went to my robe and he smirked. "I'm sorry, were you entertaining?"

"Very funny. Why are you here?"

"I think you'd better let me in," he said. "Unless you want your neighbors hearing about your dirty laundry."

Knowing that the nosey old lady next door probably had her ear to the door, I clenched my jaw and let him in. "So, what dirty laundry are you talking about?"

He pulled out his phone and showed me. It was the same picture that had been sent to me from Cole's phone.

"What's going on here, O'Brien?" he asked. "Fraternizing with the enemy?"

I gave him a dirty look. "Are you stalking me?"

"Not me. An associate."

I should have known. "That picture means nothing," I said, crossing my arms under my chest. "We were at the gym."

"Looks like he was ready to work you out real good."

"Fuck you. Get out of my apartment," I said, pointing toward the door.

"I'm sure Walters will be very interested in seeing this photo. And this one too," he replied, showing me another one, this time of me leaving Cole's townhome.

"I was interviewing him about Ronnie's murder," I replied angrily. "What, are you stalking me now?"

He ignored me. "And what were you doing here?" he asked, holding up another picture. This time it was of me on the back of Cole's motorcycle. "Looks like you've been doing much more than interviewing him."

"What do you want?" I asked coldly.

He began unbuttoning his suit jacket. "I think you already know the answer to that."

I pulled my robe in tighter. "You've got to be kidding."

"Do you know what kind of trouble you'd be in if Walters sees these photos? You'd lose your job."

"If you show him any of them, I'll make sure your wife hears the tape I made yesterday."

"You're not going to play that for her. In fact, you're going to give me the tape."

"The hell I am."

He lifted his phone and began typing. "Fine. You know, I'm tired of being married anyway. My wife is a dried up bitch who only knows how to complain. But, there's one thing for certain, I know how much you care about your job, which you won't have after I send these photos to Walters."

I held up my hand. "Hold up."

He looked at me.

"Please, don't do this."

"How much is your job worth to you, O'Brien?"

"Everything."

He grinned evilly. "And that's what I want from you. Everything."

I glared at him.

"You can start by removing your robe," he said.

"You're despicable," I said, not knowing what to do. I loved my job and the thought of being fired made me sick. The thought of him touching me made me even sicker.

Bronson unzipped his fly and began touching himself. "Come on. Show me what you got, O'Brien. I don't know what it is about you, but I can't stop fantasizing about what you've got hiding underneath your clothing."

Horrified that he was masturbating in my apartment, I shuddered. "Stop it."

"Get on your knees," he ordered, breathing heavily.

Appalled, I pointed to the door. "Get out!"

He moved in front of me and tried sticking his hand under my robe. I pushed him away and stumbled over to the coffee table. Spying my cell phone, I picked it up.

"If you don't fight, we can get this over with and I'll be on my way," he said, paying attention to what I was doing.

I pushed the camera button, turned around, and got a picture of him, his hand on his penis. His face turned red with rage. I took another one as he shoved it back into his pants.

"You fucking bitch," he growled, as I pressed a few more buttons on my phone. "What in the fuck do you think you're doing?"

"You'd better delete those pictures of me and Cole, or I'll send this one to Walters. I might still lose my job, but you won't only be fired, you'll go to jail."

He glared at me.

"And I don't know who your other stalker friend is, but he'd better delete his too."

"Fine," he said angrily. "You delete yours and I'll delete mine."

"Oh no," I said, laughing coldly. "I'm not going to delete anything because I don't trust you."

"Why should I trust you?"

"Because I could have given the audio tape to Walters earlier today, but didn't and I have integrity, which you don't."

A vein began to throb in his head. "You don't know what integrity is. If you didn't you wouldn't be screwing the biker."

"You have no proof that I screwed anyone but I have proof that you were trying to screw me," I said.

Livid, Bronson charged me. He grabbed my phone and shoved me away roughly. "You think you're so smart, you little bitch?" he sneered, pulling up the photos. He deleted them and then tossed the phone back to me. "Boom! How do you like me now?!"

Knowing that he'd try something like that, I'd sent one of the pictures to Cole. I told Bronson what I'd done and his smile fell.

"How do you like *me* now?" I said with a smirk.

"You crazy bitch," he answered. "Do you know what you've done?!"

"I know exactly what I've done and you made me do it. Now, get the fuck out of my apartment or I'll have Cole send one to Walters," I said as my phone began to ring.

"You're going to regret this," he said, grabbing his jacket. Without another word, he stormed out of my apartment.

I answered the phone.

"Who the fuck was that?" asked Cole, talking about the picture.

I explained what had happened.

"Jesus, are you okay?"

"I am now," I said, although my hands were shaking.

"I can't believe that sonofabitch tried that shit with you. Where did he go?"

"I have no idea. Why?"

"Did you call the police?"

"No. I can't. I'd have to explain what happened."

"Okay. Don't worry about him," said Cole. "I'm going to make sure he leaves you alone."

"You? What do you plan on doing?"

"Nothing you need to know about."

And this was why I had to stay clear of Cole Johnson. "You can't go after Bronson. Do you hear me?"

"Why? He went after you. He's been stalking you. He needs someone to put him in his fucking place."

"I can handle him."

He didn't say anything.

"I'm serious. Stay away from him. I'll figure something out."

"Fine. I'll stay away from him," Cole answered, his voice clipped. "If that's what you want."

I sighed in relief. "It is. You know it's better if you don't get any more involved in this than you already are."

He ignored my comment. "Do you want me to come over?"

"No," I replied, although I would have done anything to be held at that moment.

"Do you want to come back to my place?"

"I'd better not," I said, sitting down on my sofa.

"What about tomorrow? Can I see you?"

"I told you before, I think it's better if we don't see each other again."

"Is that what you really want?" he asked, sounding hurt.

No. It wasn't. But there was no other choice. I couldn't throw away my career away so easily. Not for a man I barely knew.

"Yes. It is."

Cole sighed.

"I have to go," I said, noticing that my sister was calling me.

"Terin, just... today was one of the best days I've had in a long time. I really, really enjoyed being with you."

"I enjoyed being with you, too, Cole. But–"

"I get it," he said quickly. "I want you to know that if you change your mind and want to get together again, though, I'm here."

"Thanks, Cole," I replied.

"And if Bronson gives you any more trouble, I'm also here."

I smiled. "I appreciate it. I need to take care of him on my own though."

He let out a frustrated sigh. "I know. That's the kind of woman you are. In many ways, you're a lot like my sister. Anyone fucks with her and she needs to 'handle' it."

I laughed humorlessly. "Maybe I should ask her for advice."

He chuckled.

"I have to go. My sister is calling," I said, noticing that Torie was calling back a second time.

"Okay. Call me if you ever need someone to talk to or… have a midnight rendezvous."

I snorted. "Oh yeah? You mean if I want to hook up?"

"Of course. No strings attached either."

I had to admit, sex with Cole had been the best I'd ever had. "I'll keep that in mind."

"And I'll keep up on my condom supply."

I laughed. "Okay."

"Goodbye."

"Goodbye, Cole."

After hanging up with him, I called my sister back. She'd learned about Ronnie and Pete and just wanted to chat about the murders.

"I don't know anything," I told her, feeling mentally exhausted.

"You sound tired."

"I am."

"Okay. I'll let you go and we'll talk later. We're still on for Saturday, though, right?"

"Yes," I promised her. "I'll be there."

Thirty-four

TERIN

THE NEXT MORNING when I arrived to work, as usual Bronson was there and we both ignored each other.

"Did you hear? The charges have been dropped," said Fred, stopping by my desk.

"What charges?"

"The ones against Chips and Gomer."

I frowned. "How?"

Just then, Walters stepped out of his office and called me into his office.

"Close the door," he said, not looking happy.

I did and sat down. The tension in the room told me that he was furious about something. I couldn't imagine Bronson spilling the beans, however. Especially since I had the picture of him with his hands on his pecker.

Walters opened up a file that was sitting on his desk and pulled out a photo. It was the one of me and Cole, on his motorcycle.

"Can you explain this?" he asked.

"Where did you get it?" I asked, my heart sinking.

"It was in my in-box this morning," he said sternly.

I clenched my jaw. "Was it from Bronson?"

His eyes narrowed. "No. Did he know about it?"

"Someone is stalking and taking pictures of me."

"Sorry to hear that. My question is – what in the hell are you doing with Cole Johnson?"

"He gave me a ride. I had a flat tire," I lied.

Walters studied my face. "Bullshit."

"Look, there's nothing going on between us. I swear to God. As far as this picture goes, so what, he gave me a ride."

"And what of this picture?" he asked, pulling the one of me and Cole at the gym out of the same file.

I sighed. "I know it looks bad but I had no idea that Cole was going to be there."

"So, you were trying to avoid him?"

"Yes. No. I guess I will be now," I said. "Since everyone seems to think there's something going on between us."

"Look, O'Brien. I'm not naïve. You two look like you're about ready to tear each other's clothing off," said Walters.

"Yeah, I know but if you'd been there, you have realized that it really was very innocent," I answered, lying to myself this time as well as him.

"Innocent." Walters leaned back in his chair. "Charges have been dropped against Chips and Gomer."

"Why?"

He held up one of the photos. "Because of these pictures. We can't charge them for attempted rape because their lawyer has these pictures too.

257

Incidentally, they're saying that you and Cole have manufactured this entire story because of his history with them."

"That's bullshit."

"I know it is," he answered. "But, we're pretty fucked here. There's no case now that they have pictures of the two of you together."

"What about Pete's death?"

"We know who killed Pete. We don't know who killed Ronnie. It certainly wasn't the two men who've been sitting in jail the last couple of days. We had nothing holding them and their lawyer knew it."

"So, they're free?"

"Yes. They were released about an hour ago."

I swore.

"That's not all. You're suspended for thirty days."

I sat up straight. "What?"

"You're lucky it's only thirty days. You're lucky you still have a job."

I let out a ragged breath. It could have been worse. "Fine."

He handed me a suspension form, reiterating the fact that I couldn't return to work for the next thirty days. I signed it.

"Look, I'm not blind. Something happened between you and Johnson. I don't know what it was but you'd better get your shit together if you want to keep working in this department."

"Yes, sir," I said grateful that he was giving me another chance.

Walters nodded toward the door. "Like I said, thirty days."

I stood up and walked out of the office. I went over to my desk and grabbed my purse. It was then that I saw the grin on Bronson's slimy face.

Fuck you, too.

I took out the audio recorder I had in my purse, waved it in the air so that he could see it, and stepped back into Walters' office.

"What is it?" he asked.

I set the audio recorder on his desk. "You should know how one of your male employees treats women. Oh, and also..." I pulled out my phone and showed him the image of Bronson that I'd sent to Cole.

"What in the hell is going on here?" he asked angrily.

"Yesterday, Bronson tried threatening me with the same pictures that are in your file. He wanted me to have sex with him and in return, he wouldn't show you those photos. When I told him to fuck off, he proceeded to masturbate in front of me. I, in turn, took that picture and told him that I'd share it with you if he didn't get the hell out of my apartment."

"Is that the truth?" he asked, staring over my shoulder.

I turned around to find Bronson standing back there, livid.

"It was consensual," he replied. "Until she went nuts on me and decided to take pictures."

I chortled. "Really? Consensual? I wanted you to pull that nasty thing out? You're one sick bastard."

"Don't listen to her. She invited me back to her place yesterday and begged for it."

Walters let out a ragged sigh. "Jesus, Bronson."

"He's lying," I said. "Listen to that audio and you'll hear him threatening me."

Walters nodded and looked at Bronson. "I think we'll listen to it together. Sit your ass down."

Bronson glared at me but did what Walters ordered.

"You can take off," said Walters, sounding exhausted. "I'll give you a call later."

I nodded and left.

***

Still angry and full of energy, I drove home, changed out of my work clothes, and headed to the gym. This time I stayed out of the weight room and was able to get on one of the treadmills right away. I turned on my music and began running. Fifteen minutes into my workout, I noticed someone getting onto the one next to mine. I looked over to see if it might have been

Cole, but it was another tall, dark, but not quite as handsome stranger. He smiled at me and I smiled back.

"How does this thing work?" he asked, pointing to the buttons on the machine.

"What do you mean?"

"I just want to run. I don't want to climb any hills or anything," he said, pushing buttons.

"Then you should select the 'manual' setting. That way if you want to make it incline, you can do it while you're running and then lower it when you've had enough."

"Oh." He smiled. "There's the button. Thanks."

"You're welcome."

An hour later, as I was walking out of the building I bumped into him again.

"Thanks again for the pointers. I don't know what I would have done without you."

I chuckled. "You've never been on a treadmill before, have you?"

"No. I usually jog outdoors. I figured I'd try it out, since there was a free one available. They're usually taken."

"I know," I answered. "They need to invest in some more machines."

"They really do. Anyway, I was thinking about stopping across the street to the coffee shop. Would you care to join me?"

"Thanks for the invitation, but I'm sweaty and just want to head home," I told him.

"I understand. How about another time?"

"Maybe," I replied, thinking that he seemed very nice. "Hold up, you're not in a motorcycle club, are you?"

He laughed. "Why?"

"Long story," I answered.

"I know that some of the guys from the Gold Vipers work out here," he said, looking around the lot. "Don't worry, I'm not one of them."

"Good to know."

"So, can I have you your number?"

"Sure." I gave it to him. "My name is Terin."

"Terin? Interesting. I'm Tony."

"Nice to meet you."

"You as well. So, what are you doing Saturday night?" he asked, typing my phone number into his cell.

"I actually have a bachelorette party to go to," I replied.

"Uh oh," he said, smiling. "Sounds like trouble."

"I'm sure we'll be getting into a lot of that," I answered. "We'll be bar hopping on a party bus."

"Are there going to be strippers?"

I raised my eyebrow. "I really don't know. Why?"

"I actually work part-time as a male dancer," he answered, lowering his voice.

"Really?"

"Yes. I work for a place called Stars and Stripes All Male Review. We perform live shows and also do private parties."

"Interesting," I replied. "So, you strip down all the time in front of hundreds of women and yet *don't* have a girlfriend?"

"In my line of work, you meet a lot of women, but most of them are hot for the guy they see on stage, not the person they are off of it. Take for instance, whenever I tell a woman that when I'm not dancing, I normally work in the mall, selling phone service plans, it somehow ruins it for them."

I laughed. "You're one of those pushy cell phone guys? Oh, man… that would ruin it for me, too."

He gave me a puppy-dog stare.

"Okay, okay," I replied. "I'd probably keep you."

Tony laughed. "I was hoping you'd say that. Anyway, if your plans for Saturday night change, call me. I'd love to get together with you," he said. "Even afterward. I'm a late person. We could still have coffee somewhere."

"I'll keep that in mind."

He smiled at me and took off.

"Who was that?"

I turned around to find Cole standing there and wearing a stony expression.

"A guy I met by the treadmills."

263

"What did he want?"

I frowned. "He asked for my number."

His eyes pierced mine. "Did you give it to him?"

I couldn't help but feel a little giddy that Cole was jealous.

"It's none of your business," I said, wishing that he wasn't so much more handsome than Tony. It would have made it easier for me to move on.

He gave me a cold, harsh smile. "Fine."

I started walking toward my car when he grabbed my arm, pulling me back.

I scowled at him. "What do you–"

Cole took my mouth, hard and fast. Torn between wanting to kiss him back and being angry, I pushed him away.

"What is your problem?" I asked, wiping my mouth.

A slow smile crossed his lips. "You can't replace me with a cheap knockoff. Besides, he takes steroids. You'll piss him off easily and he'll frustrate you because of his small pecker."

I laughed harshly. "How do you know he takes steroids and that he has a small pecker?"

"Because I've seen him shoot up. As for the other thing, steroids aren't penis friendly."

"I appreciate your concern, but I'm a big girl and can take care of myself."

He didn't say anything, which I was grateful for. Lately, I hadn't done a very good job of taking care of myself. He and I both knew it.

"We had a great night and I'll remember it always. But, you and I are not compatible."

"It sure felt like we were yesterday. In my kitchen. On my bed. In the shower."

The mention of yesterday's escapades made my stomach heat up. Even now I wanted him and could tell that he knew it, too. "Goodbye, Cole," I said, turning away. "Stay out of trouble."

"Where's the fun in that?" he asked, a smile in his voice.

I didn't respond but I could feel his eyes burning into my back as I walked to my car.

Thirty-five

COLE

T HE **JEALOUSY HAD** taken me by surprise. When I'd seen Terin flirting with the guy in the parking lot, I'd wanted to throw her over my shoulder, find the nearest bed, and remind her that it had been my name she'd been gasping the day before. Instead, I waited until the douchebag had left, confronted and kissed her. Even as I claimed her mouth, I could tell she was fighting the attraction she had for me with everything she had. She was so damn stubborn. All I could do was give her time and see if she changed her mind. If she didn't, I'd give her a couple of weeks and try again. I certainly wasn't ready to give up on her. Not after the mind-blowing sex we'd had. No woman had ever gotten under my skin the way she had. Not only that, she had her shit together and that was sexier than hell.

My phone rang, breaking my train of thought. I checked the screen. It was Tank.

"Hey, man. What's up?"

"Chips and Gomer have been released from custody," he said, cracking sunflower seeds into the phone.

"You're kidding me. Why?"

"I'm not sure but I thought you should know."

"Thanks."

"You should also know that he's shooting his mouth off about visiting your detective friend. I think he's planning on doing her some harm, Ice."

My stomach clenched. Over my fucking dead body. "Is that right?"

"Yep. You want any help with this?" he asked, reading my mind.

"Nope. I can handle it."

"Okay, but you change your mind, you know I've got your back."

"I appreciate it," I said.

"Talk to you later."

"Yeah."

I hung up the phone and shoved it into my pocket. I knew where to find Chips. I'd find him before he put his hands on Terin again.

Thirty-six

TERIN

W HEN I GOT into my car, I noticed that Walters had called and left a message. Bronson had been fired, but I was still suspended.

You still have your job, I reminded myself.

I called him back, mainly because I still wanted to know about the caller on the gas station video.

"They're still working on it," he replied.

"Why is it taking so long?"

"It's not a priority."

"What about Ronnie's murder? Have they figured out who did it yet?"

He didn't answer right away. When he did, I felt like someone had hit me in the gut.

"I can't share the information with you, O'Brien. I think you know why."

"Why? Does it have something to do with the Gold Vipers?"

"I can't get into it with you. You're off the case, too. For obvious reasons."

"I understand," I replied, knowing I'd disappointed him.

"There's something else you should know. You're being transferred to a different department."

I let out a ragged breath. I knew it was going to happen. I'd made it happen.

It still hurt.

"Which department?"

"Cyber Crime. You'll be required to take some Computer Investigation training courses."

"Okay."

"I'm sorry that you had to deal with Bronson. I had no idea he was such a fucking whack-job."

"I know."

"One thing you should be aware of… he was furious about being fired and because he knows where you live, I'd be very cautious."

"Thanks for the warning."

"Other than that, how are you doing?"

"I'm fine."

"Good."

"I'm sorry that I disappointed you," I told him.

"You did," he admitted. "But, I believe in you and think you deserve a second chance. Obviously, it can't be in the same department, but you still have a job with the city of Jensen."

"I do and I appreciate it," I said, my eyes getting moist.

"I know you do, O'Brien. I know you do."

***

271

I spent the rest of the week cleaning my apartment, watching movies, and working out at the gym. Fortunately, I didn't find myself running into Cole either. It was a relief, and yet, I found myself thinking a lot about him. The short amount of time we'd spent together had been one of the best times I'd had with a man. It wasn't just the sex, either. Not only did he know how to make me laugh, but he was a great listener.

When Saturday rolled around, my sister called me earlier in the day to make sure that I was still planning on attending her bachelorette party.

"Yes," I said. "Of course."

"Great. Other than that, how are things going?"

"Good," I replied. I hadn't told her or my mother that I'd been suspended.

"Any news on those murders from last week?"

"Nothing new," I replied, although I didn't really know myself. I quickly changed the subject. "So, is mom still planning on going tonight?"

"Yes," she said. "So is Frannie, I guess."

"This should be interesting," I replied.

"Yes. Especially, since there will be strippers," said Torie. "It's been confirmed."

"Really? Oh boy. Speaking of strippers, I had one ask me out at the gym."

"You're not going to go out with him, are you?" she asked wryly. "I mean, think of the diseases he probably has."

"Just because he strips doesn't mean he sleeps around," I said, although I didn't truly believe my own words.

"Of course he does. Guys are pigs, even the hot ones. I bet he's getting laid every night by a different woman."

"So why would he ask me out?"

"Because you're more of a challenge, probably. I mean, you do look like a bitch."

I snorted. "Excuse me?"

"You have that 'don't approach me' look."

I walked into my bathroom and stared at my reflection. "You think so?"

"Yes. I do, too. It's in our genes."

"Huh," I replied, studying my face. I didn't think that I looked like a bitch, not that I'd mind. I was in law enforcement. Bitchiness was a great skill to have. "I never knew."

"Who's going to tell you that you look like a bitch? Plus, you have a gun." She chuckled. "A bitch with a gun. That would scare most men all the way to China. I suppose that since he's a stripper, he thinks he's got a handle on women, though."

"He doesn't know that I have a gun," I reminded her.

273

"So, you still look like a bitch."

"Okay, I'm hanging up," I said laughing.

"Be at my place around seven. The bus leaves at seven-thirty."

"I'll be there," I promised her.

Thirty-seven

COLE

"YOU'RE FUCKING KIDDING me?" I repeated, staring in shock as Tank presented me with my new cut. We were in the chapel and I was apparently getting patched.

"This is no joke, brother," said Tank. "Put it on."

I removed my Prospect cut and handed it to him.

He tossed it into the garbage can. "Another one bites the dust," he said, closing the lid.

I looked around the room at the other members, looking for disapproval, but everyone was smiling at me.

"I don't know what to say," I said, putting it on. "This has got to be the happiest day of my life. I had no idea that it would happen, and this soon?"

Tank patted me on the back. "I know it's soon, but you earned it. Especially this week."

It *had* been an eventful week. Not only had I discovered who it was that had shot up the Devil's Ranger's party, the one that Billy had been injured at, but I'd managed to set up a meeting between Schmitty and Tank. Apparently, Schmitty had been the one who'd ordered the hit on Ronnie and was now trying to bring peace between the two clubs. Tank was still a little skeptical about it, but was willing to meet in a safe place for a peace talk.

"You know what this means?" asked Tail, smiling at me from across the room.

"What?" I asked, smiling.

"We're going to party like fucking rock stars tonight, my friend," he said. "I even got us some Cuban cigars."

"Nice," I replied, as he held them up.

"By the way, here's another gift," said Tank, throwing me a box of rubbers. "Now that you're patched, you're going to have women fighting over you and we know how unprepared you are."

They all laughed. I hadn't mentioned Terin's name, but I'd shared the condom story.

"There's enough to cover an army in here," I said, opening the box.

"I'll take some of those," said Hoss. "In case I get lucky."

"That reminds me, did you check out any of those dating sites?" asked Tail.

"Yeah, I did. You gotta pay money for most of them. Then, you meet these chicks and hope they like you. Even if they don't, it's still a free meal for them and not so much as a hand job for you. I may as well just go down the street and hand my credit card over to one of the hookers. At least it's a sure thing and I'm not getting stiffed by the end of the night."

We all laughed.

When the meeting was over, Tail and I had a beer together.

"Did you tell Raina about finding the shooters?" he asked.

"She knows," I replied, remembering the conversation. Tank and I had both sat down with her. Apparently, the guys that had shot up the party had been Independents. They'd been screwed over by Ronnie, who owed them a large sum of money. When he refused to pay, they retaliated by shooting up the party. I'd learned all of this from Chips. After Tank had informed me that he'd been released from custody, I hunted him down and beat the fuck out of him, during which he confessed to having known about the shooters all along. I forced him to tell Tank the same story. Afterward, we both spoke to Raina, who understood that there wasn't anything we could do and that involving the law wasn't an option. We all agreed that the person responsible for so much heartache was, in fact, Ronnie, who was now dead.

"So, you ready for tonight, brother?" Tail asked, clinking our bottles together.

"Damn right I'm ready."

"Congrats, man. You deserve it," he replied.

"Thanks. I just hope that everyone else thinks I'm worthy of wearing the cut," I said.

"Gonna be honest with you, Ice... I was a little unsure of you. Hell, we all were. Especially after what took place before Tank brought you in."

"Yeah, I know," I said, sighing. "That's something Raina and I will regret for the rest of our lives."

"Emotions were running high. Hell, if I had a kid and something like that happened, I'd be looking for blood too."

"Raina was in so much pain. She thought Billy was dead," I said, staring at my beer bottle. "And that Slammer had ordered the shooting."

"That's what Ronnie wanted you to think. A quick death had been too merciful for that fucker. He should have been skinned alive."

I agreed.

Sensing that I was still feeling unworthy about being patched, he leaned forward and looked into my eyes. "Ice, you're definitely one of us, man. You've got heart, soul, and as far as I'm concerned, have proved yourself. Not just by what you did this week either. I've been watching you. Everything we've had you do, whether it was cleaning toilets, setting mouse traps, or running to the liquor store before closing... you never complained. Not once. Never gave any attitude. Even better, you did what we told you to do and asked to do more. Hell, as far as I'm concerned, you're a fucking rock star."

"I wanted to prove myself," I replied, grinning.

"You did, brother. You did."

I noticed Hoss, who was playing darts with Raptor, staring at me from across the room. He smiled and raised his beer bottle.

"See, even Hoss has forgiven you," said Tail, watching the exchange.

I wanted to believe that, but in my heart of hearts, I knew that it would take a lot longer for the old man to come around. He might accept me as a member of the club, but something told me that he was only doing it for Tank's benefit.

Thirty-eight

TERIN

I **WASN'T EXACTLY** sure what to wear for the bachelorette party and settled on a pair of black jeans and a blue sequined tank top that sparkled when I moved. I carefully applied my makeup, quite a bit more than usual, and wore my hair down. I finished it off with a spritz of perfume and short high-heeled black suede boots that made my legs look longer.

When I arrived at my sister's, her eyes lit up. "You look gorgeous! I wouldn't have even recognized you. Now you don't just have a bitch face. You have a sexy bitch face."

"Thanks," I said wryly. "You look beautifully bitchy yourself." And she really did. Torie had on a little black dress, white high heels, and her blonde hair was piled on top of her head. Around her neck she wore a diamond pendant that looked like it cost more than my car.

She laughed and gave me a hug.

"Are you sure you should be wearing that?" I asked, following her into the living room.

"You sound just like mom," she said. "Relax. Nothing is going to happen to my necklace. If I do lose it somehow, it's insured."

"Okay."

When we reached the living room, my mother was already there. She was sitting with another woman I assumed was Frannie.

"Terin!" she cried, jumping up from the sofa. "Look at you. You look so pretty!"

"Thanks, mom," I said as she pulled me into her arms. "You look very nice yourself."

She stepped back and smiled down at her blue jeans and white satin blouse. "Thanks. Frannie helped me pick it out. By the way," she turned to the other woman. "I'd like you to meet my daughter, Frannie. This is Terin."

The other woman stood up and we shook hands. She was about my height, with medium length blonde hair and laughing eyes.

"I've heard so much about you," said Frannie, giving me a warm smile.

"Oh, crap," I said, smiling back. "I hope she didn't talk your ear off too badly."

"Not at all. It's been nice hearing about you and Torie. My own daughter has been away for the past three weeks and listening to your mother talk about the two of you has been refreshing."

"Where is she? Vegas?" I asked.

"Yes," said Frannie. "She was married there a couple days ago."

"You don't look too happy about it," I said, noticing that her smile had waned.

She sighed. "Don't get me wrong... I'm happy for her, just a little perturbed that they didn't invite me to their wedding."

"Didn't she say it was a spur of the moment thing?" asked my mother.

"Yes, and... they're supposed to be renewing their vows when they get back into town. I guess I'm just old fashioned," said Frannie. "I'd have liked to have been at their original wedding."

"What's your daughter's name?" I asked.

"Jessica," she replied. "Jessica Stone, now," she replied.

"The bus is here!" cried Torie, staring out the window. She turned and smiled at us. "Are you ready for a 'what happens on the party bus, stays on the party bus' kind of night?"

"Oh my," said Frannie, smiling again. "I have a feeling I'm going to need some aspirin tomorrow morning."

"That makes all of us," said my younger sister. "If you do it right, that is. Let's go, ladies!"

***

There were fifteen of us altogether, including mom and Frannie. As we stepped onto the bus, we were

284

given cocktail mugs with colorful penis straws, soft feather boas, and tiaras.

"Okay, everyone!" called out my sister's best friend, Amanda, as we put on our boas and tiaras. "You're all getting a scavenger hunt activity sheet, too." She explained that we would get points for everything that we did on the list and at the end of the night, someone would get a prize.

I stared at some of items that we could do to earn points, including dancing on a table, getting a stranger to French kiss you, and dirty dancing with two guys at the same time.

"Looks like I'm going to fail this challenge," I said dryly.

"Don't be a party pooper," said Torie.

"I'll try not to be," I said, staring at another activity. "Give your panties to a stranger? Does that mean we have to have sex with them?"

"Only if you want to," said Amanda.

"Oh my," said Mom, pointing to the list. "Am I reading this right? Get a stranger to buy you a Blow Job?"

"That's a shot," I told her.

She laughed. "Oh. I'd like to see what that looks like."

"It's actually pretty yummy," said Amanda.

"So is the shot," said my sister, winking.

"Torie," laughed Mom. "Keep that to yourself!"

285

"You wanted to come, Mom," she said, smiling. "You can only blame yourself!"

"Speaking of *coming*, we have male dancers meeting us in two hours," said Amanda, looking at her watch with a devilish smile.

"Then let the party begin!" hollered Torie, raising a bottle of champagne.

Two night clubs and several cocktails later, most of us were feeling no pain. Including my mother and Frannie, who I could tell were having a blast. In fact, by the time we were leaving for the next bar, they had almost all of their activities checked on the scavenger hunt list.

"I'm so glad you joined us!" hollered my mother to Frannie over the music.

"Me too!" she hollered back. Her tiara was crooked and her lipstick was smeared. But she wore a big smile. "I haven't had this much fun since I was in college!"

"Where are we going next?" I asked the bus driver. I'd been nursing most of my drinks, knowing that we still had a long night. I also knew that if my sister and mother were going to be getting drunk, one of us had to keep their wits together.

"Rumors," he replied.

Thirty-nine

COLE

AS PART OF MY reward for getting patched, the guys brought me to an upscale gentleman's club in downtown Jensen called Goddess. Knowing that there was a dress-code, we left our cuts behind and wore black silk seersucker shirts with the Gold Vipers emblem etched on the back. They were used for formal occasions by patched club members only.

Unfortunately, there wasn't any alcohol allowed at Goddess, so after my second lap dance, we headed across the street to Rumors for a couple of beers.

"Isn't this the place that your ex-girlfriend works at?" asked Tail as we walked across the street. There were seven of us – Tank, Raptor, Chopper, Horse, Tail, Hoss, and myself. Grover had borrowed a limo from someone who owed him a favor, and he'd dropped us off at the strip club. He was now on standby, waiting for further instructions.

"Yeah," I replied.

"You've been here before?" he asked.

"A couple of times. It's really not my thing," I answered. "What about you?"

"I've been here a number of times and usually get lucky. In fact," he grinned. "I have a hotel room on reserve up the road. Just in case."

"Won't you get charged if you don't use it?" asked Chopper, walking next to us.

"Believe me, before the night is over, it will be used. Hell," he grinned at me. "Even better idea, since this is your night, I say we get you laid first."

"I'm game for that," I answered, especially after having two strippers crawl all over me at Goddess. Funny thing was, the first one I'd selected, looked almost like Terin, only with fake tits. I didn't realize it until Tank had made a comment about it. Afterward, I selected a blonde with tats all over her body, wanting to get my mind off of the detective before I did something stupid. Like drunk texting her later.

"One thing I hate about these places," said Tank, when we walked into the main part of Rumors, which was dark, packed, and so loud we had to holler at each other. "All they play is fucking pop tunes."

"Women love dancing to this shit," said Tail, winking at two girls who were already checking us out.

"Tell me about it," said Raptor. "Adriana has it blasting through the house every fucking morning."

"Why do you let her if it irritates you?" asked Tail.

"Because she isn't a morning person and if I take that away from her, then we'll both be irritated," he replied.

"You learn to pick your battles," said Tank.

"Another reason why I'm single," said Tail. "My house. My music."

"That'll change," said Tank, smirking. "You just wait."

"I hope that doesn't happen until I'm forty," said Tail. "Until then, I'm going to fuck all the girls you can't and tell you how great it is."

Tank and Raptor both flipped him off.

"This place is crazy," said Hoss, frowning at the crowd. "Maybe we should just go to Griffin's?"

"No. This night is for Ice. He's not going to get laid at Griffin's. At least not by anyone new," said Tank.

"He's right. Relax, Hoss. You might even get laid in this place," said Tail.

Hoss's eyes lit up. "I guess it wouldn't hurt to have a couple of beers. Hell, we're already here."

"Damn, I'm so horny I can barely see straight," said Tank as we made our way through the crowd and toward the bar.

"Oh, my God, you guys are Gold Vipers? Can I get a selfie with one of you?" squealed some chick in a pair of jean shorts that had more holes than fabric.

"Here, sweetheart," said Hoss. "You can take one with me."

The chick looked at me and pointed. "I was thinking *him*. No offense. I'm trying to make my ex jealous."

"And he wouldn't be jealous of me?" asked Hoss, looking offended.

"You're just not might type. Danny would never believe that I'd hook up with you. Sorry," she said and then looked at me again. "Would you mind?"

"No," I said, amused. I moved next to her. "So, you're trying to make your ex jealous, huh?"

"Yeah. The bastard cheated on me," she said, holding her phone toward us. "I want him to see what he's missing."

I slid my arm around her waist. "Let's do this right then," I said, pulling her closer. I bit her lightly on the ear as she snapped the photo.

"Thanks," she replied, shivering. I could see fresh goosebumps on her arms as I pulled away.

"My pleasure," I said.

She checked the picture and then noticed Tail. "How about you. Can I get one with you as well?"

"Sure, but instead of playing these games, why don't you just fuck him out of your system?" said Tail, putting his arm around her. "They say that works sometimes."

She stared up at him and smiled. "Are you offering?"

"Sure, why not?" he answered. "But only if you buy me a drink first. Then you can have your way with me."

"Fair enough," she said, dragging him toward the bar.

"That lucky, fucking bastard," said Hoss, staring at them in disbelief. "Not only is he going to get laid, but she's paying for his booze, too."

"He's something else," said Tank, smirking. "I would have gotten slugged saying something like that."

"Me too," said Raptor before motioning toward the bartender. He ordered a round of beers and took out his credit card.

"I'll got the next round," said Tank.

"Damn right you will," said Raptor.

"Hoss. Check those two out. Maybe you can make a Hoss sandwich," said Tank, pointing toward the dance floor. There were two chicks grinding against each other.

"I'll even supply the Hossy sauce," Hoss answered, wiggling his eyebrows.

We all laughed.

"Holy shit," said Tank, staring in disbelief toward the other end of the dance floor. "Is that Frannie?"

We all turned to find Tank's stepmom dancing with a group of women, all of them wearing tiaras and boas.

"Looks like a bachelorette party," said Raptor, handing out beers as the bartender gave them to him.

"That's right. She mentioned it to me the other day and I completely forgot that it was tonight," said Tank just as Tail walked back over to us, alone.

"What happened?" I asked. "You were just about to make use of the hotel room."

"Apparently, her ex just showed up. If I'm going to get laid, I'd rather find someone without baggage," he said, ordering himself a beer.

"No shit," I replied and then saw a familiar face on the dance floor.

Terin.

She was with the bachelorette party.

"What's wrong? You look like you've seen a ghost," said Hoss, now standing next to me.

"Nothing's wrong," I said, unable to tear my gaze away from Terin. She looked sexier than hell, and damn if the woman didn't know how to move her hips.

"Look at Frannie go," Tank said, chuckling. "I wonder if she ever got down like that with my old man."

"The woman has skills," said Chopper, also smiling.

"Of course she does. Women over forty have lots of skills," said Tail, paying for his beer.

"Let me guess – your first lay was a woman over forty and you'll never forget the experience," said Hoss dryly.

"No, but I *have* had two twenty-year olds at once," he joked, shoving his wallet back into his jeans. "And I'll never forget that."

"So, you've never had a woman over forty?" asked Hoss.

"Honestly, not until tonight," said Tail, heading toward the dance floor with his beer.

"Don't you dare!" hollered Tank.

Tail looked back at us and smiled wickedly.

"I swear, if he tries hitting on Frannie, I'll kick his ass to kingdom come," said Tank, taking a swig of his beer.

"I think she can take care of herself," said Raptor.

"He'd never fuck her," said Horse. "She's untouchable. He knows that."

"Actually, check it out, I think he's going for the bride," said Raptor, pointing.

Sure enough, Tail had entered the circle of women and was now dancing with the blond wearing the mini veil. His hands were around her waist and they were both smiling at each other.

"Hope she's not supposed to be virgin or the groom is going to be in for a big surprise on their wedding night," said Hoss, taking a swig of beer. "Especially after Tail gets done with her."

"If he's not careful, she'll be *pregnant* by their wedding night," said Tank, chuckling.

Frannie, recognizing Tail, began to laugh. Then she turned and saw us watching by the bar.

"Oh, here she comes," said Tank. "Best behavior, guys."

We knew the drill. Tank loved Frannie like a mother and wanted us to be respectful around her. None of us had any problem with that, considering she was one of the nicest women around. Plus, my nephew now called her grandma, which meant that she was indeed the matriarch of the family.

"What are you boys doing here?" she asked, after making her way off of the dance floor.

"Ice was patched tonight," said Tank, putting his arm around my shoulders. "We're whooping it up."

"Congratulations," she said, beaming a smile at me. "I know how much this means to you."

"Yeah. It means a lot," I said, grinning humbly.

"What in the hell is *that*?" asked Tank, pointing to her drink. There was a straw that was shaped like a penis.

Frannie took a drink from it and grinned. "Isn't it great? We all got them."

Tank laughed and put his arm around her. "You behaving yourself, Ma?"

"Probably a lot more than what you boys are," she answered.

"What are you talking about? We been as good as choir boys," he replied.

"Since when do choir boys wear perfume?" she answered, wrinkling her nose.

Tank's face turned red. "Uh, Tail bought me a lap dance over at Goddess."

"You'd better make sure Raina doesn't smell that on you when you get home or you're going to be in big trouble," she replied, looking amused.

"I didn't do anything wrong. I didn't even touch the girl," he replied, holding his hands up. "Here, smell my hands."

"Uh, I'll take your word for it," said Frannie.

"He's right. You really can't touch the strippers," said Raptor.

"Is that what you're going to tell Adriana?" she asked. "Because if you are, you're going to need to douse yourself with vinegar to get rid of the stench of that perfume. Good Lord, do they shower in it?"

"Apparently," said Raptor, smelling his shirt. "Don't worry, Adriana doesn't get jealous. She has no reason to."

"Neither does Raina," said Tank.

"I wish I had someone at home who'd get jealous," said Hoss, sucking in his gut. "Hey, hot chicks coming this way. Ten o'clock."

Frannie looked over her shoulder. "Oh, hey... here comes my friend Tracy. She's the one who invited me to the bachelorette party."

We turned and saw a woman around Frannie's age heading toward us. Behind her was Terin. Our eyes met for a brief second. Recognizing me, she looked ready to bolt.

Forty

TERIN

WHEN I SAW Cole, I couldn't deny it. As much as I wanted to believe that he meant nothing to me, my pulse raced knowing that he was only a few feet away.

"Tracy and Terin," said Frannie, when we approached. "I want you to meet my stepson Tank and his friends." She then proceeded to introduce us both to the bikers.

"We've met," said Cole, staring at me, an amused expression on his face.

"Yes," I replied, my eyes dropping to his clothing. He wore a black, short sleeved dress shirt that emphasized his muscular frame. If it were possible, I thought Cole looked even more handsome than ever.

"You've met? Oh," said Mom. "Are you the young man who helped her at the deli last week?"

"Yes he is, Mom," I said, answering for Cole.

"Thank you," she said, her eyes softening. "For helping Terin. I don't know what would have happened if you wouldn't have showed up."

"I would have been fine, Mom," I said, a little too firmly.

"I'm sure you would have but… you have to admit, it was very kind of him. He could have went on his way and stayed out of it. But he didn't."

"Yes, he could have walked away." I glanced at Cole. "She's right. Thank you, for your help," I said, feeling as if everyone was staring at me.

"Like I said before, it was my pleasure," he said, his mouth twitching.

"I love those new shirts, Tank," said Frannie, as if somehow knowing that it was time to change the subject. She touched the fabric of his. "I'm so glad you let me order them for the club. You boys look so handsome."

"Even me?" asked Hoss.

Frannie chuckled. "Yes, Hoss. Even you."

Tank turned around to show us the Gold Viper insignia on the back. "They are nice. We decided to wear them tonight, since we were celebrating Ice being patched. Some of the places downtown don't allow vests."

"Who is Ice?" asked my mother.

"I am," said Cole, surprising me. He'd never mentioned that he had a road name.

"Why do they call you Ice?" she asked.

"Not too sure myself," he replied with a goofy smile.

"It's that cold stare of yours," said Hoss, smirking. "Especially when you need another beer. Tank, order another round of beers."

"Ice gets that same look his sister has when she is pissed off," said Tank. "When she gives it to me, I know I've done something wrong."

"Raina has beautiful eyes," said Frannie. "So are yours, Cole. I mean, Ice."

"Thank you, Frannie," he replied, winking at her.

"He does have very light blue eyes," said my mother, who was obviously feeling very well from the alcohol. "Almost the same color as my Husky's, Bailey. Don't you think, Terin?"

"Yes." I replied, remembering how intense they were when he was fucking me. The memory woke my lady parts up downstairs.

"Thanks," he said, staring at me while he took another swig of beer.

"So, you've been patched? What does that mean?" asked my mother.

Frannie explained.

"Oh. Well, congratulations. You must be thrilled."

"I am thrilled and honored," he said. "One of the happiest nights of my life."

"Hey, did I just overhear that you were patched tonight, Cole?" asked one of the waitresses, walking over. She was dressed in a short miniskirt and a tank top that read "Rumors." It was tight and barely covered what could only be fake boobs.

Cole tensed up. "Yeah,"

"Why didn't you call me?" she asked, stopping in front of him.

He shrugged. "I didn't know you'd be interested."

"Of course I'm interested! Silly."

He didn't reply.

"Well, this calls for a shot. What do you say?" she asked, batting her eyelashes up toward him. "Will you let me buy you one?"

Cole sighed. I could tell that he was irritated, however. "Sure, Patty. Why not?"

So *this* was Patty.

My stomach clenched with an unexpected jolt of jealously.

"I'll be right back," she said, touching his arm possessively before walking away.

"Patty looked like she wanted to eat you alive," said Tank, smirking. "Watch out. That shot might have a roofie in it."

"No shit," said Cole, smiling grimly.

"Maybe I should take it for you," said Hoss. "I'd let a girl like that do anything she wanted."

I was about to tell them that roofies were nothing to joke about when Patty came back.

The next thing I knew, she was planting a shot between her breasts and thrusting her chest out toward him.

"Really?" he asked dryly.

"Oh shit," said Tank, chuckling.

"What's wrong? You chicken?" goaded Patty, staring up at him.

"Of course he's not chicken," said Hoss. "Take it, Ice."

Cole glanced at me.

I looked away.

"Come on, Cole. You know you want it," she said, squishing her breasts together so the shot would stay in place. "Remember, don't use your hands."

"What are you waiting for?" asked Hoss. "Get in there before someone else takes the shot."

"What is it?" Cole asked.

"A slippery nipple," said Patty. "I know how much you like those."

My mother, who'd been unusually quiet, giggled.

Cole gave me one last look before leaning over Patty's chest. He pulled the shot out of her cleavage with his lips and sucked it down. Then he slammed the shot glass onto the bar. The guys cheered.

"How was it?" asked Hoss, patting him on the back.

"Not bad," said Cole, wiping his mouth. "A little sweet."

"Ready for a second?" asked Patty. "I've got another one coming up with your name on it. Or, maybe you'd rather have a Blow Job?"

The guys all laughed.

"Are we talking a shot or the real thing?" asked Hoss.

"The shot," said Patty. "Although, I do get off in another hour, Cole. Wink. Wink."

Hoss choked on his beer and wiped his mouth. "How can anyone pass that up?" he asked in a raspy voice.

Feeling sick to my stomach, I turned toward my mother. "This place is giving me a headache," I told her in a low voice. "I'm going to go outside and get some fresh air."

She gave me a concerned look. "Okay. Do you want me to come out with you?"

"No thanks," I said, turning away. "Stay here. I'll just go sit on the bus until I feel better."

"Alright, dear."

"Is she okay?" asked Frannie.

"She'll be fine," I heard her say as I walked away.

I hurried through the night club and stepped outside. As I made my way over to the bus, someone tapped me on the shoulder. I turned around and saw that it was Tony, the guy from the gym.

"Oh, hey. What are you doing here?" I asked, surprised.

"You're never going to believe it," he replied. "I think I'm actually dancing for your bachelorette party!"

"How did that happen?" I asked, noticing that he was wearing army fatigues.

"Someone called in sick and they asked me if I was free. Since I didn't have a date tonight," he said, winking, "I told them I could do it. I have to admit, I was hoping it was going to be your bus."

"Really? You were hoping... So, I get to see you naked and we haven't even been out on a first date," I teased.

He laughed. "No shit. Well, you could keep your eyes closed... although, you might not want to."

"I think I'll keep my eyes open. Just so I can watch my mother and the other girls throw dollar bills at you."

"Let's hope they do. Maybe we can use the money afterward? An early breakfast?"

"Maybe," I replied. He seemed nice, although he was obviously conceited.

Tony looked over my shoulder. "Can I help you?"

"Yeah. Take a hike," said a deep voice behind me.

Stiffening up, I turned around to find Cole standing there. He was all danger and hard muscles, ready to strike. It was both frightening and sexy as hell.

"What the fuck did you just say to me?" asked Tony, staring back at him with a scowl.

"You heard me," he replied in a rough, dark voice.

Sensing that the situation was about to get ugly, I stood between them. "Just... hold up. Cole, what do you want?"

He looked down at me and his face softened a bit. "I want to talk to you."

"Talk? Why? I thought you were busy inside, getting a blow job?" I said curtly.

"That's not what I wanted from her. Hell, I don't want anything from Patty. I told you that before."

"So, you just want to talk?"

"No. I want more than that," he said, his eyes smoldering with frustrated need.

Oh God.

He was horny.

So was I.

"We'll talk about this somewhere else," said Cole, grabbing me by the hand. He started pulling me with him, away from the bus.

"Wait a second. I can't just leave with you! Let me go," I demanded, trying to pull away.

"You'd better let her go, buddy," said Tony, following behind us.

Cole stopped abruptly and turned on his heel. Still holding my arm, he addressed Tony. "This doesn't concern you, *buddy*," he said. "And the only reason I'm not kicking your ass at this moment is because you serve our country."

"Actually, it's just a costume. I think," I said, not understanding why I was telling him. It could only make matters worse. "Isn't it?"

"Yes, but that's not the point," snapped Tony, looking angry. "You can't force a woman to do something she doesn't want to do."

"Terin, am I forcing you to do something you don't want to do?" Cole asked me, his eye boring into mine.

My heart began to race as I realized that more than anything, I wanted Cole to whisk me away and fuck the hell out of me. Maybe it was the alcohol. Maybe it was the thought of him and Patty together and I was jealous. Or, maybe, I just missed the hell out of Cole *(Ice)* Johnson. I wasn't sure. I just knew that I wanted to leave with him and screw everyone else.

Wait, I'm no longer in that department, I thought.

"No. You're not," I said, unable to look at Tony.

"Crazy broad," mumbled Tony, turning and walking away.

"Hey... hey... hey... What's going on out here?" asked Torie, walking quickly toward me with Amanda.

"I'm leaving," I said, giving her an apologetic smile. "You don't mind, do you?"

"What do you mean you're *leaving*?" Noticing that Cole was holding my arm, my sister frowned. "Wait a second, who in the hell are you?"

"I'm a friend," he said, turning on the charm. "Don't worry, I'll make sure she gets home safely."

Torie looked at me in disbelief. "I can't believe you're leaving. What about the strippers?"

"I don't think I'll be missing them," I replied as Cole pulled my back against his chest and I could feel his raging hard-on.

"Wait a second, aren't you with the Gold Vipers?" she asked.

He smiled. "Yeah."

"And you two are leaving together…?"

I nodded.

"As in hooking up?"

My cheeks grew warm. "I… I don't know. We're just going to talk."

"Right." She grinned. "Hell, if anyone needs to get laid, it's you. Have fun."

"Thanks, you, too," I replied. "Tell Mom I'll call her tomorrow."

"You'd better call me tomorrow, first," she said. "If I'm letting you leave my party, I need details. Okay?"

"We'll see," I answered.

She looked at Cole. "Damn, I hope the strippers are as hot as you are."

"Stop, you're making me blush," joked Cole.

Torie laughed and then dragged Amanda away.

"You ready to get out of here?" he whispered into my ear.

"I've been ready since you drank that slippery nipple," I told him.

Growling in the back of his throat, he grabbed my hand and led me away from the bar.

Forty-one

TERIN

"**W**HERE ARE WE going?"

"Over there," he said, nodding toward a hotel.

"A hotel?"

"Yup. Tail reserved a room earlier."

I stared at him surprise. "Tail?"

"Yeah. He said we could have it."

"Won't he need it?"

Cole smiled. "He'll figure something else out. He's very resourceful."

"He told you that we could have it? How did you know I'd agree to even go there with you?" I asked, stopping abruptly.

Cole gave me a devilish grin. "I knew right away when I saw how pissed off you were at Patty."

"Pissed off? I don't know what you're talking about," I said innocently.

He barked out a laugh. "Liar."

***

Ten minutes later, our clothes were lying next to the bed and his tongue was between my legs, wiggling

310

and teasing my clit. Whenever I came close to the edge of an orgasm, he would stop.

"You want me to make you come, Detective?" he asked.

"Yes," I begged.

"Isn't that against department policy?" he asked, sliding his finger inside of me.

"I don't care," I whispered.

"Are you going to arrest me if I don't?"

"Maybe. Yes... Maybe..." I whimpered as he began teasing me again with his tongue.

"What if I don't want to go to jail?" he said, stopping.

I looked down at him. "Are you really going to make me suffer all night?"

"You made me suffer. I wanted to fuck you last night. The night before. And the night before that," he said, inserting a finger into my other hole.

I gasped.

Staring up into my eyes, he began stroking my clit again with his tongue while his fingers played me like a piano. The pressure built quickly and this time, he was merciful enough to take me all the way. My hips convulsed as I came and I cried out in both relief and ecstasy. Before I had time to recover or catch my breath, Cole flipped me over, grabbed my hips, and entered me from behind.

"You going to come for me again, Detective?" he said, wrapping my hair around his fist. He pulled my head back and leaned over me, his other hand cupping and squeezing my breasts.

"Mm… yeah," I said, reveling in the way his cock filled me. He pulled out slightly and began thrusting in and out, hitting my G-spot. Soon, I was having another orgasm, my womanhood contracting around his cock and making him gasp in pleasure as he exploded inside of me. When he was spent, Cole collapsed on top of me.

"Can you stay?" he whispered, smoothing the hair away from my face.

"Yes," I replied, closing my eyes.

He held me in his arms and we both fell asleep.

Forty-two

COLE

I **WOKE UP** several hours later to the sound of my cell phone ringing. Terin and I both sat up.

"Sorry," I said, grabbing my phone.

"Who is it?" she asked, yawning.

"Tank," I said, answering it.

"Brother, I need to talk to you. Some shit has come up that you need to know about."

"What do you mean?" I asked him.

"Just… get to the clubhouse."

"Now?" I asked, looking at the clock. It wasn't even nine a.m.

"Yes. Now," said Tank.

I sighed. "Okay. I'll be there as soon as I can."

"Okay," he said and hung up.

"What's wrong?" asked Terin, as I rolled out of bed.

"I don't know," I replied, heading toward the bathroom. "Club business I think."

"What did he say?"

"That he had some stuff to talk to me about. I'm sorry. I was hoping we could at least have breakfast."

"It's okay."

I looked back at her. "Don't worry. I'll get you home. Just don't leave."

She stood up and started grabbing her clothing from the carpet. "I won't. I couldn't even if I wanted to."

"I'll call someone for a ride."

"Thanks."

An hour later, we were in Dover's truck.

"Where to?" he asked.

Terin gave him the directions to her apartment building. It was about twenty minutes away from my own place.

"Thanks," she said, opening up the door.

"Wait. I'm going to walk you up," I told her.

Half expecting her to protest, I was pleasantly surprised when she agreed.

***

Terin lived on the top floor of her building in a one-bedroom apartment.

"Can I stop by later?" I asked, glancing around her place. It was warm, inviting, and she had a big screen television that was larger than the one at my place. I pictured us curled up on her sofa, watching it together, among other things, and silently cursed Tank and his timing.

She nodded. "Yeah. Call me first. I might not be around."

"Why not? You have a date with soldier boy later?" I teased.

"He hasn't called me yet, so I'm not sure," she replied with a smirk.

I grabbed Terin around the waist and pulled her into my arms. "You'd better hang up if he calls."

"Why?"

"You'd be an accomplice in a murder case."

She laughed. "Is that right?"

"Hell yeah. He tries going out with my girl and the blood will be on your hands."

She cocked her eyebrow. "Your girl?"

I smoothed the hair away from her eyes. "My woman? Does that sound better?"

Terin let out a ragged sigh. She looked away.

I tilted her chin back up, forcing her to look at me. "You can't deny that there's something pretty powerful going on between us. And, I'm not just talking about sex."

"Yeah," she replied. "I can't."

"So, what are we going to do about it?" I asked, rubbing her cheekbone with my thumb.

"What do you want to do?"

"Spend more time with you. A lot more time."

Terin smiled grimly. "Well, since I've been suspended, that shouldn't be too difficult."

My eyes widened. "Suspended? Why?"

"My boss, excuse me my ex-boss found out about us."

"How and what do you mean EX?"

She explained that someone had sent the photos to Walters. Someone who'd been working with her coworker, Bronson.

"Isn't that the same guy who showed up here and tried raping you?" I asked angrily.

She nodded.

"That fucking pile of shit. I should hunt his ass down and–"

"No," she said firmly. "You'll end up in jail."

"It would be worth it."

"Seriously, Cole, don't do anything to him. I mean it. Besides, maybe it was for the best."

"Why would you say that? You've been suspended."

"But not fired, which I'm grateful for. I've also been transferred to Cyber Crime. I'm not part of the team investigating you or your club anymore."

I stared at her in surprise.

She smiled.

"So, we can see each other?"

"That depends," Terin said, staring into my eyes. "You see, even though I'm not in the department anymore, I'm not about to date anyone that I can't trust.

That means I can't be with you if you're going to be involved with anything criminal."

"I'm not," I replied. Which was the truth. Sure, I'd beaten a few guys up, including Chips. But, I didn't have a record and wasn't planning on creating one.

She cocked her eyebrows. "You're now an official member of the Gold Vipers."

"It's just a motorcycle club. There's nothing illegal going on, Terin."

She stared at me for a few seconds. "Did they have anything to do with Ronnie's death?"

"I swear to God, our club had nothing to do with it."

"You're not lying to me?"

I frowned. "No. Absolutely not," I said sternly. "I wouldn't lie to you. You've got to believe me."

She relaxed. "Okay."

"Babe, I want to be with you but you have to trust me. I know you're a cop, and I'll respect that, but getting grilled over and over about something that I'm definitely not a part of is exhausting."

"Sorry. It's a force of habit," said Terin.

"I get it, but, all you have to do is ask me once about something and I'll tell you how it is."

"Okay."

"So, are we going to do this?" I asked her.

"You mean be together?"

"Yeah, I mean be together."

318

"We can try it. See what happens."

I grinned. "Good."

My cell phone went off again.

It was Tank.

"Shit. I have to go."

"One more thing," she said. "If I ask you about the club and what they expect from you, you'll be frank?"

"If I ask you questions about your job, can you always be frank?" I countered.

"That's different."

"Not in the club's eyes." I sighed.

She frowned.

"Look, you want to know what they expect from me? Loyalty, trust, and commitment."

"That's all?" she asked, a little dryly.

They also expected confidentiality, but I didn't feel it needed to be said. Something like that was obvious. "Yes and I promise that you can expect the same thing from me."

"Okay. I guess I can't ask for too much more than that."

"Babe, I definitely have more to offer you," I said, smiling wickedly. "And we'll discuss that later tonight."

Terin smiled. "I'll be waiting."

319

Forty-three

COLE

W HEN GROVER AND I arrived at the clubhouse, I was surprised to see that Tank, Raptor, and Tail were also still wearing the clothes they'd had on the night before. They were all standing next to their bikes and talking.

"What's going on?" I asked, noticing their grave expressions.

"We got a situation. It's not good," said Tank. "Follow me. Be prepared, though. We've got a little bit of a drive."

"Okay," I replied.

Tank nodded to the others and they all got onto their bikes.

"I wonder what's going on?" asked Dover, as we followed them away from the clubhouse in the van.

"You don't know either?"

"No. I have no idea."

Forty minutes later, we were driving down a dirt road, two towns over from Jensen. When we finally stopped, it was at a secluded cabin in the middle of the woods. I got out of the van and walked over to Tank.

"Who owns this place?" I asked.

"Hoss," he replied, removing his sunglasses.

"Where is he?"

"Inside," said Tank. He looked over at Dover. "You can take off."

"Won't Ice need a ride home?" asked the prospect.

I stiffened up, wondering the same thing. Warning bells were going off in my head. Something was obviously up. The other guys were barely looking at me and it made me wonder what the hell was going on and if I was in trouble.

"He'll have one. Don't worry about it," replied Tank.

"Okay," said Dover. He started the van and we watched as he turned it around and disappeared back through the woods.

"Come on," said Tank, walking toward the cabin.

I followed him inside, the others behind me. He led me into the kitchen, where Hoss was sitting. His hands were tied to a chair. If that wasn't shocking enough, standing next to him at the counter was Walters, Terin's old boss. He looked totally relaxed and was drinking a cup of coffee.

"Hey, Cole. How's it going?" asked Walters.

"It was fine until I walked into here. What in the hell is going on?" I asked, stunned.

"You want to tell him or should I, Hoss?" asked Walters.

Hoss scowled. "Fuck you. I'm not saying a thing and I want a lawyer."

"This isn't an arrest," said Tank. "A lawyer won't help you."

"Your old man is probably turning in his grave," spat Hoss. "Marrying his murderer and patching her brother? You should be ashamed of yourself."

I couldn't believe the hostility in Hoss. I knew he and Slammer had been best friends but had no idea of the rage he obviously had toward me and Raina.

"How many times do I have to tell you – Raina wasn't targeting Slammer personally," said Tank. "She wanted to strike back at who she thought had killed Billy. She was distraught."

"Do you think it makes it any easier to stomach?" asked Hoss. "A brother of ours was killed. Not only that... *your* father!"

"Yes. *My* father and if anyone is still grieving, it's me," said Tank, looking beat. "But, I'm not going to hold this against Raina. I've forgiven her even when she hasn't forgiven herself. I think you should do the same."

Hoss sighed. "I'm sorry, son, I just can't."

"Why not? It was a crime of passion," interrupted Walters. "Look inside yourself right now. Imagine that you had a son and thought the leader of the Devil's Rangers was responsible for his death. You think you'd react any different?"

"Damn right I would have," he said in a not-so-convincing voice.

"Bullshit. You'd have gone into their clubhouse, guns blazing," said Tank.

"Hell yeah, he would have," said Raptor, speaking up for the first time.

"Maybe, but I'd have at least made sure who it was that needed to be punished beforehand," said Hoss.

"Ronnie pointed his finger at Slammer. Made us believe that it was him, even when he knew it wasn't," I said.

"That was your first mistake. Believing that fucker," he replied.

"And why wouldn't he?" said Tank. "Ronnie was the V.P. and we all know that club brothers are supposed to trust each other. What does that say about you?"

Hoss couldn't meet his eyes.

I looked at Walters, still stunned that he knew about Raina and me. Obviously, Terin didn't know or she'd have said something. "So, you're not going to turn my sister in?"

"No. I've known all along that your sister killed Slammer. Tank told me," replied Walters.

I looked at Tank.

"Walters is on our side. He grew up with my old man," he explained. "He's even cleaned up a few messes that Dad made over the years."

"Are you sure that nobody else on the police force knows about Raina or my involvement?" I asked.

Walters sighed. "Just Bronson. I don't know if you remember, but someone called in a tip last week. Bronson took the call."

I wagged my thumb at Hoss. "Let me guess, from him?"

"Yeah. He's the one who spilled the beans about Raina shooting Slammer," said Walters. "He also took some photos for Bronson, apparently. Of you and Terin. They've been working together."

"That was you?" I asked Hoss, clenching my jaw. "You were following us?"

Hoss didn't respond.

I took a deep breath to calm down. "So, what happens now?"

"We were going to ask you the same thing," said Tank. He leaned against the counter. "Since he's trying to have your ass thrown in jail, what do you recommend?"

"I have no idea," I said, feeling sick to my stomach. "What about Bronson? Where's he at right now?"

"Don't worry about him. Bronson is out of the picture," said Walters. "He was fired a couple of days ago. Drank his sorrows away and ended up in a fender bender."

"He's in the hospital?" I asked.

"He's dead," replied Walters.

I stared at him in disbelief.

Walters nodded. "It's true."

"Lucky for him. Walters told me how he tried assaulting Terin," said Tank. "And bribing her to have sex with him. If you ask me, the pile of shit got off easy by dying behind the wheel."

"She mentioned that he'd shown up at her place and exposed himself. Even sent me a picture to use against him. I was going to kill the bastard, but she wanted to handle it her way," I replied.

"Terin handled it the right way by bringing me the proof I needed to fire him," said Walters.

"Karma got him in the end," said Raptor. "I guess that's one less mess we have to worry about."

"You still have this one though," said Walters, finishing up his coffee. "And... guys... I don't want to know what happens next. So, I guess that's my cue to exit."

"Thanks again for letting me know about Hoss and Bronson," said Tank.

"I figured you'd want to know that you had a stool pigeon in your club," he replied.

Hoss grunted.

"How did you find out that Hoss was the one on the video?" I asked.

"I recognized him," explained Walters.

"Does Terin know anything about this?" I asked.

"No. Two days ago, I told her that the video was too shoddy to identify anyone. I knew that your club would want to handle this situation. The less she knows, the better."

I nodded.

"Hoss," said Walters, walking over to him. He put a hand on the old man's shoulder. "I know your hurting because of Slammer. We all felt his loss and are going to miss the hell out of him. But, you of all people know that wherever he is, Slammer has forgiven Raina. He also knew that she wasn't going after him personally. You're the only one who doesn't see that."

Hoss just sat there quietly with a stubborn look on his face.

Walters sighed. "Okay. If you're going to take care of this the way I think you are, don't leave me any fucking evidence."

"Don't worry. It's all good," said Tank, shaking his hand.

Then Walters was gone and it was just the club.

"What are we going to do?" asked Tank, looking at me. "It's your call."

I looked at Hoss. He suddenly looked like a lonely, frail old man. I pulled up a chair next to him and looked him in the eye.

"Just like my sister wanted vengeance for Billy, you wanted it for your friend. I get it. I understand it. I can't even blame you for trying to find a way to settle the score."

He nodded curtly.

"And, hell," I went on, "you could have even tried killing one of us, but you didn't. You just wanted us to do time. I'm actually thankful for that."

"There's been enough bloodshed," he mumbled. "I wasn't looking to shed anymore."

"Exactly. And there's also been enough rage and sorrow." I looked around the room at Tank, Tail, and Raptor. I knew that as much as Hoss had gone behind their backs too, this group loved him. It was obvious by how grief-stricken they looked at the thought of harming him. Nobody wanted Hoss dead. Hell, as angry as I'd been, even I didn't. I told him as much.

Hoss still wouldn't look at me, but his eyes filled with tears.

"If this is really up to me, I'm going to show you the same compassion that Tank showed us." I looked at our president. "Let him go."

Hoss gave me a surprised look.

"You sure?" asked Tank, frowning.

"I'm positive. As far as I'm concerned, everyone in this room has been a victim. It needs to end here and now," I said firmly.

"He's right," said Raptor. "We have to work through this. It's what families do."

"Can this be worked through, Hoss?" asked Tank, his voice softening. "Can you learn to forgive Ice and Raina?"

Tears trickled down Hoss's cheek. "I suppose that if you can, there's no reason why I should be holding a grudge like this." He looked at me. "I'm sorry. I fucked up. I acted without thinking things through and I realize that now. Kind of like Raina, I guess."

"You know what Uncle Sal always says? When life throws you lemons, you make lemonade. But without the sugar, it's still hard to swallow."

"What's the message there?" asked Tank, scratching his chin.

I chuckled. "I don't know. Make sure you carry around sugar packets?"

Tail, who'd been quiet, laughed. "I think it just means that life is never going to be easy and to suck it up."

Tank unlocked Hoss's handcuffs. "You know we weren't actually going to kill you, right?"

"I wasn't sure what to think," he answered, looking both humiliated and ashamed. He brushed at his tears.

"Don't get me wrong, I'm still pissed as all hell that you tried putting my fiancée in jail," said Tank. "You're going to have to make up for that, big time."

Hoss nodded. "I know."

Tank sighed. "You really going to let this shit go now, Hoss? If you can't, then you'll have to walk away from the club. You realize that?"

"Yes, I do. I'd rather die than walk away," he replied. "You're my family."

I held out my hand to Hoss. "Friends?"

He stood up and hugged me. "Brothers. And, I'll make it up to you," he said, patting me on the back. "I really will."

"You don't have to," I answered. "Just, the next time you have a beef with me, tell it to my face."

He nodded. "Yeah. I will."

"We all good now?" asked Tank, looking around the room. "Anyone else got something they want to get off their chest?"

"I think we're all good," said Raptor, looking at his watch. "Which is more than I can say for me when we go home. I'm expecting Adriana to be waiting for me with a gun and a shovel."

"You guys haven't been home yet?" I asked.

"No," replied Tank. "Tell you the truth, I'm not looking forward to doing it either. I forgot to call her."

I grunted. "Shit. Call her now or you'll never get any sleep when you get home."

Tank grinned wickedly. "Actually, I'm okay with that."

"I don't know. You might find that all of your stuff is sitting on the front lawn," I replied.

"Nah. She's getting all hot and pissed off. It'll make for some great makeup sex," said Tank.

"I didn't need to hear that," I said, giving him a pained expression.

He laughed.

"Speaking of siblings," said Raptor. "Ours are due back today. Jessica and Jordan."

"Do they need a ride from the airport?" asked Hoss.

Tank's smile fell. "What time is it?"

"Eleven thirty," said Raptor.

Swearing, Tank headed toward the front door.

"Let's just hope that my brother really did retire from mercenary work," chuckled Raptor as Tank took off.

TEN MONTHS LATER....

Forty-four

TERIN

FRANNIE STARED PROUDLY at her daughter Jessica, who stood with Jordan under the wedding arch, behind their newly built home. It was July tenth and a gorgeous day for renewing their vows in front of family and friends.

"I now pronounce you husband and wife," said the pastor, smiling at the beaming couple. "You may kiss the bride."

Jordan pulled Jessica into his arms and twirled her around as they kissed. Everyone stood up, clapping and cheering for the happy couple.

"This reminds me of the day that I married Slammer," Frannie said, holding Carissa, Jessica and Jordan's newborn daughter. "Except we were in Hawaii and our children were all grown up."

"That was a great day," said Tank, standing on her left. He grinned at the memory. "I don't think I'd ever seen Pop so happy."

Frannie smiled. "That made two of us. I think today he'd have been over-the-top with joy as well. There's so many things to be thankful for, including this little nugget."

Carissa slept on, a pacifier in her mouth as Frannie rocked the infant in her arms.

"Can I hold my cousin?" asked Sammy, Adriana and Raptor's three-year-old son. He stood on the other side of Frannie on his tippy-toes.

"She's sound asleep," said Adriana, putting an arm around her son. "Why don't you wait until the wedding is over and she needs a bottle? I bet you can help with that."

"The wedding *is* over," he grumbled. "They just kissed."

"He's right. It is over. I need to check with the caterers and make sure that everything is ready." Frannie looked at Tank. "Can you take her?"

"Me? Why me?" asked Tank, taking a step back. "Have Adriana do it."

"Adriana is already carrying two babies," said Frannie, nodding toward her stomach. She was six months pregnant and carrying twins.

"What about Raptor?" asked Tank.

Raptor snickered. "What's wrong? You scared of a little baby?"

"Are you kidding me? He's terrified," said Raina. "Ask him how many times he's held his niece."

"I just don't want to hurt her," Tank explained. "She's the size and weight of the steak I ate last night."

"Just take her," said Frannie, holding Carissa out toward him. "Or you're not eating anything today."

"Fine," he grumbled, reaching for her.

"Watch her neck," said Frannie. "Here, hold her like this." She positioned Carissa into his arms, making sure that he wouldn't drop her and then stood back. "There. See, it isn't so bad, is it?"

"She's waking up," he said, looking pale. "What if she cries?"

"Relax, you both are doing fine," said Raina, patting him on the back. She smiled down at the baby. "Oh man. I forgot how small they are."

"Small, meaning they're easy to lose," said Tank. "With my luck, I'd lose one of these things between the seat cushions of our sofa."

"Things? This is your niece," said Raina, laughing. "Not loose change."

Frannie also laughed. "I'll be back in a few minutes. Try not to panic too much, you big scary biker."

"Just make sure that when you come back, you bring a diaper," he replied, nodding toward Carissa's face, which was scrunched up and turning red.

"It's probably just gas. I'll bring one though," said Frannie, walking away.

"Oh crap. Literally. Do you guys smell that?" said Tank, chuckling.

"I think she just had some gas," said Raina. "Otherwise, she'd be screaming her head off to get changed. Is her bottom warm from pooping?"

Tank patted it. "No. I think you're right. Must just be gas. At least she feels better now I guess. Phew. Nice push, Carissa."

"Just like you to blame someone else for your swamp ass," said Raptor, chuckling.

"Mine would smell a lot worse," Tank said.

"She must feel very comfortable with her Uncle Tank," said Raina, touching Carissa's cheek gently. The baby was awake and staring at him curiously.

"Just don't you get any ideas," said Tank. "I'm not letting you have one of these until you let me set a wedding date."

"Did you actually just say that? You're not letting *me* have one of those?" said Raina. "Are you forgetting who has to keep reminding you to use protection?"

"Protection from what?" asked Billy, grabbing Raina's hand.

"From your mother," said Tank. "She can be really scary."

Billy nodded his head. "I know. Remember when you took me for ice cream without asking her. She got really mad."

"Yeah, I remember," said Tank, giving Raina a sideways glance. "Let's not bring that up. Okay, Bud? I'd like to sleep in my own bed tonight."

"We could pitch a tent in the backyard again. That's was fun," said the boy.

Tank wiggled his eyebrows at Raina. "I'm hoping to pitch a tent in my own bed tonight."

Raina snorted. "Billy, remember you're having a sleepover with Sammy?"

Billy's face lit up. "Oh, yeah."

Sammy moved over to stand by him. "We can build a fort in my room and pretend we're camping."

"Sweet!" said Billy.

The pastor motioned for everyone to move toward the reception area, to celebrate with the bride and groom."

"So, you two haven't yet set a date?" asked Adriana, as everyone moved toward the other side of the house.

"Not yet," said Raina.

"Yeah, why buy the cow when you can milk it for free," grumbled Tank.

"Don't you *even* go there. I don't milk you for anything," said Raina, giving him the stink eye.

"That's the problem. I've got backup and it's making me blue."

"Okay, T.M.I.," said Raptor, grimacing.

"What does he mean?" asked Sammy.

"It just means that Tank is... pouting," said Raptor, ruffling his son's blonde hair. "Don't ever be a Tank."

Standing next to Cole, I smiled at their exchange. I had to admit, they were an interesting group of people.

338

Fortunately, they'd opened their arms and hearts to me and I could now understand what Cole saw in them.

He put his arm over my shoulders. "You've been awfully quiet. Are you doing okay?"

"I'm doing great," I replied, smiling at him.

He leaned over and kissed me. "Thanks for coming. This really means a lot to me."

"Of course. I wouldn't miss it."

"I love you," he said,

"I love you, too."

We'd admitted our love for each other several months ago. I didn't know exactly where the relationship would lead, but I knew one thing was for certain – we were very happy.

"If you want, we can skip out early and go for a bike ride later," Cole whispered in my ear.

I'd taken his advice and had learned how to ride a motorcycle. I was now fully licensed and had been riding for about six months. Besides sex, it was one of our favorite past times.

"Won't they be angry?" I whispered back.

"No. I don't think so. We just have to stick around for a while and pay our respects," he said.

"We should at least stay for dinner," I replied. "Don't you think?"

"Yeah. We should," he answered, kissing my temple.

We stayed for dinner and were about to leave, when some of the bride and groom's friends began to make toasts. Afterwards, Jessica stood up and called all of the women over to the side.

"I almost forgot to throw my flowers!" she proclaimed, turning around.

I stood in the back of the group, not really wanting to catch the bouquet, mainly because I wasn't quite ready for marriage. I knew that if it happened, Cole would be the one standing next to me. But, we were both young and had plenty of time.

"Okay, here goes!" Jessica flung the flowers over her head and I stared up at the sky as they headed directly toward me.

Crap.

Fortunately, another young woman reached up and grabbed the bouquet before they hit me in the head.

"Got it!" called Cheeks, grinning. She turned to her boyfriend, Levi, who I heard worked at Griffin's. She held up the flowers.

"Looks like you'd better start shopping for rings," hollered Tank, smiling at Levi.

Levi chuckled. "Looks like I'll be asking my boss for a raise soon."

Tank raised his glass. "I'm sure he'll help you out."

I watched as Cheeks rushed over to Levi and sat on his lap. They were a cute couple and I could tell that marriage would definitely be in their future.

"Why didn't you grab the flowers?" asked Cole, when I walked back over to our table.

"I don't know. I guess I could have but, face it, Cheeks is dying to get married."

"And you're not?"

"I don't know," I replied, smiling at him. "I mean, when it happens it happens. I don't think we have to rush into anything."

"We rushed into sex and that turned out well," he teased.

Cole had a point.

***

Two hours later, we were on our motorcycles and enjoying the open road. Grinning from ear to ear, I followed Cole out of town, until we reached an overlook that gave us a great view of Jensen. We pulled over and took off our helmets.

"Isn't it beautiful?" I asked, staring at the lights below. "I love Jensen. I can't imagine living in a big city with all of the hustle and bustle."

"I love it, too. And even more, I love you," he replied, grabbing my hand.

341

I leaned over and kissed him. "I love you, too. Ace," I said.

He grinned. "It's Ice. Not Ace."

I stared at him. "I know. You just don't come across as an 'Ice' to me."

"That's because you've made me nothing but happy. Piss me off, though, and once glance will turn you to Ice."

"Piss me off and I'll turn you over and frisk you."

"I'd better start pissing you off more," he teased.

I chuckled.

He reached into his pocket. "I know you like to be in charge, Detective," he said, pulling out a ring box. "But, something tells me that I'm going to have to be the one who steps up to the plate."

My jaw dropped as I realized what he was doing.

Cole opened the box and pulled out a beautiful diamond ring.

"Are you sure about this?" I asked him, my throat closing up as he slid the ring on my finger.

He looked at me. "I've never been so sure in my life. So, what do you say? Will you marry me?"

My eyes filled with tears. "This means forever, you know."

"Does that frighten you?" he asked, his lip curling up.

"Everything frightens me a little," I replied. "I mean, come on. I'm a cop. I'm also a realist."

"Then you must recognize real love," he said, putting my hand on his chest. I could feel his heartbeat. "And how much I have for you."

"I love you, too," I told him.

"Then, you'll marry me?"

I nodded.

Smiling, he kissed me deeply.

"Wait a second," I said, pulling away slightly. "Does that mean you'll have the right to call me your Old Lady and I won't have any say? Because you know how I feel about that. It just *ain't* going to happen."

He laughed.

Cole had tried calling me that before and I'd told him where to go. I was two years older than him and didn't need to be reminded of it.

"I'll call you whatever you want," Cole said. "As long as you'll marry me."

"You've got a deal," I said, kissing him on the lips again.

Forty-five

RAINA

WHEN THE WEDDING was over, Adriana and Raptor took Billy home with them so that Tank and I could spend some quality time together. This basically meant loud, dirty sex in almost every part of the house. When we were both spent, we lay together in bed, like most nights, talking.

"It was nice to see your Uncle Sal today," said Tank, rolling to his side. "He's looking well."

Uncle Sal had ended up getting his liver transplant and had gotten out of the hospital the month before. "Yeah, he's doing pretty well. Hopefully he'll stay sober and not ruin his new liver."

"He has friends and family that can support him," said Tank. "Plus, now that I've sold Griffin's, we can run Sal's together."

Tank had sold the strip joint to Hoss a couple of months ago. I'd been surprised when he told me what he'd planned on doing. I'd also been relieved. I hated knowing that he had to spend so much time there. Some of the girls were skanky and I'd even seen them hit on him. He'd ignored their advances, but it still had pissed me off.

"Yes. Thank you for that."

He kissed my forehead. "Of course. You know, I'm always going to be here for you, right?"

I nodded and then cleared my throat. "So, I was thinking… maybe we should set a date."

Tank's jaw almost dropped out of his face. "For our wedding?"

"Yes. I was thinking that we should do it in Hawaii. Like Slammer and Frannie did. As a tribute, you know?"

Tank's eyes glittered in the darkness. He grabbed my hand and squeezed it. "Frannie will appreciate it."

"Okay. Then it's settled. Now, we just need to set a date."

"Yeah. Let's set a date," he said, sitting up in bed. "When were you thinking?"

"Well…" I gave him a little smile. "We have less than nine months."

"Nine months? Okay, that works for me. Wait a second." His eyes widened. "Why nine months?"

I put my hand on my stomach. "I don't know if it's the water in this damn town, or what, but if we wait any longer, we'll have an extra person at our party and if he eats as much as his poppa, we're in trouble."

Tank looked like he was about to faint.

I gave him a reassuring smile. "Don't worry. If you can handle a group of scary bikers, you can handle a little baby."

"They don't cry or wear diapers. Scratch that. Hoss probably does both."

I laughed.

He grabbed my hand and slid his fingers through mine. "So, you're certain?"

"I took a test."

"Twins?"

I chuckled. "You really don't have any experience with pregnant women, do you? It's way too early to tell. Besides, twins usually run in the family. Neither of our families have them."

"Twins don't run in either Raptor or Adriana's family. If he can produce twins, my little guys can create triplets," he proclaimed, puffing out his chest.

"Let's just worry about one baby right now. Besides, I'm the one who has to carry your kids and something tells me that one will be the size of a watermelon."

"I was pretty big," admitted Tank. "My old man told me that I weighed almost eleven pounds when I was born."

I cringed. "You're kidding me."

"No. So, when will we know if it's a boy or girl?" he asked, touching my stomach.

"In about four months. I'll have an ultrasound and they'll tell us."

"Okay."

"I was thinking that we should name the baby after your father," I told him.

He smiled.

"What was his real name?" I asked.

"Edgar."

"Edgar?"

"Yeah."

"Oh. What about his middle name?" I asked.

"Lee."

"Oh thank God," I replied.

"What's wrong, you don't like Edgar?" asked Tank, smirking.

"It's fine," I lied. "I mean, we can call him Edgar, if it's a boy but if it's a girl, we should call her Lee."

He motioned toward his manhood and gave me a cocky grin. "It will be a boy. My sperm only produces boys."

THREE MONTHS LATER...

Forty-six

TANK

"**I**T'S A GIRL," said the doctor, scanning Raina's stomach. It was her four month checkup and he was finally doing the ultrasound.

"It is?" I said, my eyes filling with tears.

"Yes," he replied and then explained how he could tell. "I mean, there's a chance I'm wrong, but in this case, I think it's safe to say that I'm probably right."

"A girl. That's great. She's going to be beautiful," I said huskily. I imagined myself, sixteen years later, meeting my daughter's boyfriends with a gun in one hand and a bat in the other.

"Are you crying again?" asked Raina, dryly.

"No. I just got something in my eye," I replied, brushing away the tears.

Raina chuckled. "Doc, you might want to check Tank's stomach to make sure he's not pregnant, too. He's been so emotional lately."

"It's my hormones," I joked, pretending to sob. "They're so out of whack!"

"It's pretty common to have partners go through similar emotions as the mother," said the doctor, printing up the pictures from the ultrasound. "Many of them even gain weight, too."

I patted my stomach, which Raina said was turning into a daddy pooch. "It's her fault. I'm always running to the grocery store because of her cravings."

"Bullshit," laughed Raina. "I haven't had hardly any cravings. In fact, I just finally stopped getting morning sickness."

"You two. I tell you," said the doctor, smiling in amusement. "I'll be right back."

"Okay, doc," I said, as he left the room.

"So, it's a girl," said Raina, studying my face.

I grinned. "Yep."

"And not twins."

"Nope."

"You're not upset?"

My eyes widened. "Upset? Why would I be upset about that?"

"Because you wanted a boy."

"Babe, we have a boy. Billy. I'm thrilled that we're having a girl. I mean, you saw me. I almost lost it here in front of the doctor," I admitted. "Hell, I'm the happiest man in the world right now. I have everything I want and am getting a daughter now? What more could I ask for?"

Her eyes filled with tears. "I'm sorry that your dad isn't going to be around to see his granddaughter."

"Not this again," I said, rubbing my forehead. Raina was still distraught about Slammer. "Listen to me, he's here. He's here right now, probably handing out cigars to all the other ghosts with a proud grin on his face."

She smiled sadly. "You think so?"

I grabbed her hand and kissed her knuckles. "I *know* so. Now, let's enjoy this moment and not talk about the past. It is what it is and you have to get over it. You feel me?"

"I feel you."

"Good," I said, staring into her eyes. "Because we are in the 'here and now'. Honestly, if things didn't happen the way they did, we wouldn't be sitting here and I wouldn't be the happiest father in the world, waiting to meet my daughter."

She frowned. "But, he'd be *here*–"

"Stop," I demanded, putting a finger to her lips. "You don't know that. None of us can predict the future. I know one thing that's for certain, though… us. You, me, our children. The club. All of my brothers and their wives. We're one big family and nothing can change that. Not even death."

She sighed.

"Raina, we don't know what tomorrow brings. Nobody does. So, let's live for today. Not yesterday. Hell, not even tomorrow. Let's live right *now* and enjoy what is and not what could have been. Can you do that for me?"

"Yes," she answered, staring at me with so much love that I felt it in my own chest.

"Good. I love you, babe."
"I love you, too," she replied.

Forty-seven

ADRIANA

"**D**ID YOU HEAR? Tank and Raina are having a girl," I said to Trevor, who was helping me feed the twins, Tara and Maya. They'd just turned a month old and already a handful.

"I heard," he replied, burping Maya.

"I think it's wonderful. Our girls will grow up together."

"Yeah. Around Tail's son," said Trevor, dryly. "Don't forget that."

I laughed. Tail and his girlfriend, Lauren, also had a young child. One who'd just started crawling. His name was Drake and he looked like his father more and more every day.

"Are those two ever going to get married?" I asked.

"I don't know. Tail loves her but he's paranoid about tying the knot."

"She's a nice girl."

"Yeah. Too nice for him," he said.

"He loves her though," I said. "You can see it in his eyes."

"Yeah. He does. Almost as much as he loves himself."

I chuckled. "No, really? He doesn't seem conceited."

"He's gotten better," admitted Trevor. "I think Lauren's tamed him."

"If she'd tamed him completely, they'd be getting married," I replied.

"You women and marriage," said Trevor. "You know, you can still love someone without the fancy wedding or certificate."

I gave him a dirty look. "So, you regret getting married?"

"No. God no," he said, giving me a horrified look. "You're the best thing that's happened to me. You know that."

"Good, because I was going to say…"

"I just mean, marriage isn't for everyone. And, that's okay."

I nodded. "I know. You're right."

"I still can't believe your brother did it," I replied. "It was such a surprise."

Trevor laughed. "I think that was probably the only time he was ever terrified in his life. And then he did it again and in front of everyone. That man has balls."

"You have balls," I told him, nodding toward our girls. "Not everyone can produce these little gems in twos."

"I've mastered the art of fornication. What can I say?" he replied, smiling proudly down at his daughter.

"Let's just hope Sammy doesn't. At least until he's an adult," I replied.

"Between him, Billy, and Drake, I think the town of Jensen is going to be in trouble in about eighteen years."

"Eighteen?"

"Okay. Sixteen. That's when I started chasing girls."

"Now you're going to be chasing *your* girls," I replied. "Away from the boys."

"Let's hope they're like you. The twins."

"What do you mean?"

"You played hard to get."

"I was hard to get."

Trevor grinned.

"What?"

"For most men. You couldn't resist this guy," he said, wagging his thumb at himself. "You let your guard down and fell hard. Admit it."

"You're right," I replied, smiling. "You were scary but charming. Bossy, but romantic. Stubborn but lovable. I couldn't resist you. I still can't. Even when I'm as mad as hell."

He stood up with Maya and walked over to me. "That goes for both of us, babe." He kissed me on the lips. "I love you, Adriana."

"I love you, too, Trevor," I told him.